Invitation to a Waltz

Invitation to a
Waltz

BEVERLY C. WARREN

DOUBLEDAY & COMPANY, INC.

GARDEN CITY, NEW YORK

1983

All of the characters in this book
are fictitious, and any resemblance
to actual persons, living or dead,
is purely coincidental.

Library of Congress Cataloging in Publication Data

Warren, Beverly C.
Invitation to a waltz.

I. Title.
PS3573.A769I5   1983   813'.54
ISBN 0-385-18398-4
Library of Congress Catalog Card Number 82-45563

Invitation to a Waltz

CHAPTER 1

"I'm not a monk, Laura! Nor a celibate priest!" the tall, good-looking man exclaimed. "Come on . . . after all, this isn't the nineteenth century. Men and women have relationships beyond a mere handshake and a brotherly kiss. And I know you're as attracted to me as I am to you. Admit it, Laura!" The young blond man gathered the frail girl into his arms and his probing lips crashed down on hers hungrily.

Her two hands pushed violently against his chest while she frantically twisted her head from side to side, trying to sever her lips from his. In one desperate thrust, she freed herself.

"Peter, whatever has gotten into you?" Laura's eyes were wide in naked astonishment at this unexpected reversal of his usual placid behavior.

"Gotten into me?" he laughed. "Nothing that hasn't been there all along, my love. Come on, relax." He grabbed for her again but she eluded his outstretched hands.

"Please go, Peter." She turned away from him; she could no longer face him or his demands.

"Laura," he said, softly caressing her shoulder with his hand. "This is the twentieth century. Men and women who find themselves attracted to one another satisfy their needs. You won't be the first."

"Attracted? What about love, Peter? What about love?" she angrily pleaded. "You said you loved me!"

He laughed derisively. "Oh, come now. You really didn't fall for that old line, did you? It was just part of the game."

"A game? You call almost a year a game?" Her voice was strident as she tried to assimilate his cruel words.

"Time is not a factor when one has a definite purpose in mind. The capture of the quarry is the crux of the game." His eyes sparkled malevolently at her.

"I suppose I was the quarry you speak of," said Laura with as much detachment as she could manage under the circumstances.

"Was? You still are, my dear. I know you love me and it will only be a matter of time before you cast off your puritanical cloak and come eagerly into my waiting arms."

"And just what am I supposed to find in your waiting arms?"

"Ecstasy beyond your wildest imagination." His grin was lurid, almost obscene.

"And after I have succumbed to your charms, what did you have planned?" Her eyes narrowed with wary scrutiny.

"Planned? Why, nothing. But I suppose I'll have to give up some of my lesser lady friends if you prove to be as fiery as I think you are, for all your straitlaced attitudes. Or are you some sort of Victorian throwback?"

"And suppose I am?"

"Then I'll have to teach you the wonders of modern life." He came up behind her and placed his hands firmly on her shoulders, nuzzling his cheek against hers, as he pulled her close to his body. "I can show you delights you never dreamed of, sensations you didn't know existed," he whispered hoarsely in her ear.

Tears were starting to well in the back of her eyes. What she thought had been a beautiful romance was disintegrating into nothing more than a sordid affair. She pulled free of him and went to the door of her apartment and, opening it, said, "Peter, I think you had better leave." Her voice rang with more authority than she really possessed.

"Is that what you really want?" he asked softly.

"I was in love with you, Peter, or thought I was," she stated, while in the back of her mind she thought this was all a bad dream and she would soon awake to find the gentle, kind Peter she had known trying to rouse her from this horrible nightmare.

Mistaking the wistfulness in her eyes and the softness in her voice for a belated surrender, Peter reached out behind him and closed the door with one swoop of his hand.

"Darling." He started toward her, his handsome face aglow with a supposed victory.

"Get away from me," she growled viciously.

"What do you think life is, Laura? Some sort of fairy tale? Are you waiting for the noble prince who will worship you from afar? Well, things just aren't that way. Not in this day and age."

"Then I don't want this day and age."

"Look . . . what harm will it do? We both want each other."

"Somehow I don't think I want you anymore. I was flattered by your seemingly selfless attentions. I was under the delusion that you were in love with me. Now I realize it was only an ego trip on my part."

"Laura, remember the time we—"

"I remember nothing, Peter. My mind is quite numb."

"You can't go waltzing through life as if it were some precious fantasy."

"I'll handle my life in my own way and time. Now, if you don't go, I'm going to scream my head off."

"If I go now, lady, you'll never see me again, understand?"

"Then . . . I'll never see you again," she answered, her voice subdued, empty sounding, her eyes averted from his.

He stared at her long and hard, his fists clenched tightly at his sides. He turned and left, slamming the door behind him with such force the pictures on the wall of her apartment gave a little bounce.

That scene had burned its way into her brain like acid over the past three years, causing her to bury herself in work, in anything and everything that would further her career, vowing no more romantic commitments. Though it came as a shock, it wasn't Peter's demand for intimacy that had upset her, even though she wasn't truly prepared for that kind of relationship. It was the idea that he had had other girl friends while declaring that she was the only one in his life. It numbed her sensitivities and left her empty. She continued to have occasional dates with men but she never trusted the motives of her male companions. She decided that no man would ever make a fool of her again, much less a quarry.

Laura thought back over her whole involvement with Peter. He was two years older than her, twenty-four when they first met during classes at Pratt Institute and found they had most of the same interests. They began meeting socially with more and more frequency. She grew fonder of him as his warm and affectionate kisses demanded nothing more of her than to return that affection, which she did ardently. And when he vowed his eternal love, she took him to meet her parents in Vermont.

Laura had had a rigid upbringing by her staunch Yankee parents. They wanted her to marry and raise a family when she graduated from college. But Laura was intent on having a career and, against her parents' wishes, came to New York City seeking employment, her Bachelor of Fine Arts in her hand. She never dreamed they would hire her when she applied at the Brooklyn Museum for a position the second day she was in the city. For once she was in the right place at the right time. They had just lost two of their employees and Laura was the answer to their prayers.

And now, after she'd worked there for three years, a position for an assistant curator became available. Laura was very pleased when out of twenty-five applicants, she received the post. Her master's from her night classes at Pratt helped greatly. At twenty-five Laura Bickford was the youngest person ever to achieve the coveted position of assistant curator of late nineteenth-century and early twentieth-century American art for the Brooklyn Museum. She reveled in it, burying her first brush with what she thought had been true love deep in the inner recesses of her being. Even her new position could never eradicate the pain of being only another filly in Peter's stable of loves, but it did give her a sense of self-satisfaction and helped to ease the hollowness that had been plaguing her.

To her astonishment, the first assignment was a rather exciting and important one. She was to catalog all the artifacts, paintings and sculptures of the remarkable Evans Mansion, located in the Thousand Islands of the St. Lawrence River. And to actually be doing this in the mansion itself was beyond her wildest dream.

Fully packed and duly on her way to begin the task, she drove her little VW Beetle along the Hudson River. When she passed Albany and the New York Thruway veered west, the boredom of driving began to set in. She had to think about something pleasant or she'd start dozing off. Her mind wandered with growing excitement at the prospect of completing a catalog all by herself. It was the first real challenge the new job afforded her and she knew there were many treasures of Americana at the Evans Mansion.

She remembered when John Donaldson, her boss, first told her of the assignment, and a smile crept across her pretty face.

"As you have seen from the pictures, Laura, Evans Mansion is a magnificent structure. When the previous owners put it on the market some twenty years ago, then abandoned it, it fell into a horrible state of disrepair until it was purchased some three years ago by its present owner, Nathaniel G. Harte."

"The famous artist?" Laura interrupted.

"One and the same. He is not only a fine and prominent artist but also a shrewd investor. The mansion is a veritable treasure-house of American Impressionism and many other objets d'art of the period. It will be an opportunity for you to observe firsthand the works in your special field. That is why I chose you for the job."

"Since he's an artist himself, I'm surprised he doesn't do his own cataloging."

"He neither has the time nor the temperament for it. Besides, he wants it completed by the middle of June."

"June? Any special reason?"

"Yes. He intends to open the mansion to the public as a museum for two or three months of the year. Everything must be presented to the insurance company in precise order before he can let the public in. He's most anxious to have it done and, I must say, is paying quite handsomely for it with a rather large endowment to our museum. I expect your very best work and want you to get everything done on time, Laura."

"You can count on it, Mr. Donaldson. And as that particular period is my field of study, there won't be too much research to do. I know most of the pieces by heart. Will Mr. Harte be at the mansion?"

"I understand Mr. Harte will be touring Europe this spring looking for fresh ideas. You will bring your work to me and I will see to it the insurance company receives it in time. Fully annotated, of course."

"Of course. When do I leave?"

"It should take approximately six weeks to complete the assignment. Let me see. . . ." John Donaldson studied the gold-framed calendar on his mahogany desk and lightly rubbed his chin. "It's now the second week of April. I should say in about two weeks. Is that any problem?"

"No. It's fine with me."

"I'll have my secretary make the necessary motel arrangements."

"Motel? I thought I'd be staying right in the mansion. Isn't it on an island?"

"It is. Unfortunately, the mansion isn't set up for housekeeping. For example, to my knowledge there are no cooking facilities there. No . . . I thought it best you stay at a motel in Alexandria Bay. From there, the island is about ten or fifteen minutes by motorboat. We'll also make sure you have someone to ferry you back and forth to the island. Any further questions, Laura?"

She snapped back to reality when a sign whizzed by stating it was only thirty miles to Syracuse. Suddenly she was hungry. She had forgotten all about lunch. She pulled into the next rest stop where all services were available. Hastily she ate a tasteless sandwich and devoured a dish of tasty potato salad—all washed down with two cups of strong black coffee. She filled her car with gas and was on her way again, sated and flushed with renewed enthusiasm. At Syracuse she turned off the Thruway and headed north toward her destination, the Thousand Islands.

By the time she reached the motel, she was physically and spiritually drained. All those hours of solitary driving had taken their toll. All Laura wanted was a hot shower and a bed to stretch out on.

The motel was inauspicious. But then, she thought, the museum was extremely conservative, especially when it came to spending money on what they considered nonessentials. Her motel and meals did not have top priority by museum standards. But she really didn't care. There was too much exultation in her for her to be concerned with the machinations of existence.

It was shortly after seven in the evening when she awoke from an unexpected but satisfying sleep. She dressed hurriedly and asked at the desk where she could get a good, reasonably priced dinner, then proceeded to walk to the recommended place.

The dinner was good and the price was reasonable. As she lingered over her coffee, Laura noticed a good-looking man staring at her. When their eyes met, he smiled at her with a crooked, impish grin on his boyish face. Laura quickly looked away and stirred her coffee absently. She was too tired and had too much work to do to be bothered with flirtatious hopefuls. Besides, the episode with Peter still bruised her mind and she had no intention of going through that again.

She was startled when the well-built figure slid into the seat across from hers.

"I'm Kevin Courtney and you must be Laura Bickford." His voice was pleasantly deep.

Laura's mouth dropped open and her eyebrows arched. "How . . . how did you know?"

"The museum informed me you'd be staying at the White Clover Inn and the White Clover Inn always recommends Sally's for meals. I hung around on the chance you would show up. I must confess, I expected some fifty-year-old dull toothpick of a spinster, not a honey-blond goddess." He smiled warmly at her.

She had no control over the bright red spots spreading across her cheekbones. No one had ever called her a goddess before and the flattery embarrassed her.

"I'm sorry if I rattled you," Kevin apologized. "It seems I know a lot about you and you know nothing of me. Let me rectify that immediately. A notice was placed at the marina stating some museum was looking for a boat to ferry one of their employees back and forth to the Evans Mansion. I answered the bulletin, my price was right and I got the job. Simple, isn't it? Sorry if I overwhelmed you. All I wanted to know was what time you wanted to leave in the morning."

Laura quickly recovered her senses. "Would nine o'clock be convenient?"

"Whatever you say, fair lady." He smiled.

"Where is the marina?"

"Two blocks down from here," he replied waving his hand to the left and rising. "See you at nine sharp."

"Yes. And thank you, Mr. . . . ?"

"Courtney. Kevin Courtney. But call me Kevin, everyone else does."

Laura watched the lean, rugged man leave the restaurant while a little voice inside her brain kept saying, "Watch out!"

Promptly at nine, Laura, wearing a camel-colored skirt of wool, white tailored blouse, sensible shoes and a cashmere cardigan to match the skirt briskly approached the marina.

Kevin looked appraisingly at the slim figure of the girl coming toward him as he leaned against one of the pier's posts. His sandy hair was tousled by spurts of gusting wind. A wry smile cracked across his face as he watched her come down the weather-worn wooden steps toting an abundance of paraphernalia. Satchels were slung over each shoulder while she tried to maintain her balance with a large briefcase in one hand and a large square box in the other. He rushed up and relieved her of some of the burden.

"Thank you." Her clear amber eyes smiled in gratitude at him.

"My, you are prompt. Have you had breakfast?"

"Yes. About an hour ago."

"Well, climb aboard and we'll be off." He extended his hand as he climbed down into the boat. Laura took it eagerly, not being used to the sway of the boat on such rough water.

"Are you a fisherman?" she shouted as the roar of the engine increased and they cut out into the river.

"Good Lord, no. I haven't the patience for it."

"Do you make your living by ferrying people about then?"

He gave a short laugh and looked at her with a twinkle in his eye. "I'd starve to death. The money's not too bad during the tourist season but that lasts only a couple of months and most of the people around here have their own boats. No . . . I design and build boats. Had my own business when I was twenty-nine. Been hard at it for three years now and haven't gone broke yet."

"Funny, I always thought all boats were made something like cars, in a factory on an assembly line."

"A lot of them are. I cater to the ultra rich who want custom design and custom features on their boats. Ever been up this way before?"

"No. What do most of the people do around here for a living? On the way up, everything seemed a bit bleak. I didn't notice any factories or shopping malls."

"Farm, for the most part. You'll find a lot of dairy farms around. And a lot of the places here are summer homes for the very wealthy."

Laura studied the scenery around her, noticing an island here and there and several shoals. "Why do they call it the Thousand Islands? It doesn't seem possible there could be a thousand islands here."

"Actually, there are over seventeen hundred islands in the river. Remember too, it's a long river. Any rock or shoal with a tree on it is considered an island, regardless of its size. What you see here is only a fraction of the river. If you'll look just ahead as we go past this island, you'll see Evans Mansion."

In minutes, the many-gabled and turreted structure loomed on the high ground of a large island like an eternal monument to a bygone era.

Kevin cut the motor and let the boat glide up to the dock. He hopped up on the wooden planking, rope in hand, and secured the boat before helping Laura out. A shudder of excitement ran through her as she automatically resumed her burdens while Kevin's hand steadied her step onto the dock. She didn't notice the tender look he cast her way as she stared single-minded at the mansion up the grade before her. Mesmerized, she headed for it when Kevin's voice drew her up sharply.

"Don't you want to know if I'm coming back for you?" he teased, displaying white even teeth in a broad grin.

"Oh, yes," she replied absently. "What time?"

"Six all right?"

"Fine. I'll be here." Once again she started for the mansion. Impulsively Kevin strode after her.

"Will you have dinner with me this evening?" he asked hopefully.

"I'm sorry. I couldn't possibly have dinner with you. I have a tremendous amount of work to do and I'm on a tight time schedule."

"Please. You have to eat sometime tonight and I'd like to show you about town. I insist." His smile was beguiling and Laura felt herself weakening—and she did have to eat.

"Perhaps. Let me see how well I progress today," she replied, returning his friendly smile.

He undid the rope and jumped into the boat. "Till tonight, then," he called, switching on the motor.

The incline up to the mansion was steep but the strain was eased by polished marble steps. Laura looked down at them and realized what a tidy sum they would bring on the New York market.

Reaching the entrance, she set down her briefcase and camera case to fumble in her purse for the key Mr. Donaldson had given her. The key shook in her hand as she opened the door.

The reception room was a wonder of marble, translucent white marble, which continued up the wide central staircase, the latter graced with filigreed black wrought-iron railings. The high plastered ceiling was a profusion of elaborate floral designs crowned by a gilded chandelier whose dangling crystals shimmered with reflected light. Laura was duly dazzled and could well imagine what the rest of the mansion had in store for her if the entry hall was this breathtaking. She made a mental note of the several alabaster statues and the two large Chinese vases.

Her mind reeled at the opulence as she wandered through the reception and drawing rooms. She entered the impressive dining room located behind the main staircase and when she pushed apart two sliding doors in the dining room she was greeted by a spacious ballroom. Laura's vivid imagination took over as she envisioned a mass of swirling people gliding around the marbleized floor to the strains of a Strauss waltz. The images of voluminous, colorful gowns swishing around like sparkling jewels amid the formal black male attire set her pulse racing. She sighed deeply, lost in a dream world of yesteryear.

The growing weight of her equipment brought her back to reality as the ache in her shoulders increased. She relinquished her mental wanderings and went to the door on the far side of the ballroom. She wanted to at least walk across it even if she would never waltz on it. To her relief, the door opened on what she believed could only be the library. Without a second thought she decided to make it her base of operations and deposited all the photographic equipment on the floor, except her camera. She had saved and done without a lot of things so she could purchase the very best, and she carefully placed it on the huge, highly polished mahogany desk, then flung her briefcase up beside it.

"Well, now," she said aloud, triumph ringing in her voice. "I'll have a look at the second floor before mapping out my procedure."

Her voice sounded strange to her in the large, empty house, yet for all intents and purposes, the house seemed to have a lived-in quality about it. There was an intangible humanity to it that precluded utter desertion. She shrugged and headed for the main staircase.

The second floor was a maze of varicolored and period-decorated bedrooms and sitting rooms. Twelve bedrooms and baths in all. She had counted them deliberately. From the notes she had, she knew the third floor was an exact duplicate of the second. The attic floor contained the servants' quarters with a few guest rooms. For the lesser guests, she supposed, and smiled to herself.

But, as John Donaldson had told her, she needn't concern herself with either the third or attic floors. They were not furnished and there was nothing there to catalog. In fact, he had gone out of his

way to tell her that Nathaniel Harte didn't want anyone poking about
up there, as only the first two floors would be open to the public.

Laura thought she would have a look up there anyway before she
became immersed in her work. Besides, she was halfway up already.
On the third floor, all the doors were locked as she roamed the narrow hall. Finding no access to any of the rooms, she climbed the
stairs to the fourth floor, the attic.

There she found herself in a small reception parlor, which was un-
furnished and had wide french doors that opened out onto an observation deck. She was delighted to find they were unlocked and
opened easily under her hand. Eagerly she ventured out onto the
railinged balcony.

From its high vantage point, she could see downriver for some distance. The river was wider than she had thought previously, and
what had appeared to be land masses from the boat turned out to be
long, narrow islands. She placed her arms on the wrought-iron railing
encircling the deck and gazed dreamily at the impressive scenery.
The docile wind blew her medium-length honey hair gently about her
face and the golden strands sparkled as the sun bounced in and out
of the clouds. At last she roused herself from the self-imposed trance
and went back in. Testing the two doors leading out of the parlor,
she found them locked. This time she couldn't even gain entrance to
a hall. Considering it an ill omen signaling a return to work, she
compressed her full lips in a grim smile and went back downstairs.

She opened her overstuffed briefcase, took out some papers and
the floor plan John Donaldson had given her and placed them on the
desk. She reached into one of the satchels and brought forth a tall
thermos of coffee, one of two she had purchased at the restaurant
that morning along with some sandwiches.

She sat down, poured some coffee into the plastic top, then turned
her attentions to a specific plan of procedure.

The morning and the better part of the afternoon went by quickly.
Laura was so absorbed in the work before her, she literally jumped
out of the chair when a loud crash echoed down from upstairs. It so
unnerved her, she called "Who's there?" several times before she realized her small voice would not carry up to the confines of the floors
above her.

When she went up the grand marble staircase this time, she was
oblivious to the luxurious surroundings. The only thing on her mind
was the reason for that horrible noise and the fact there was a possibility she wasn't alone in the mansion when she had been given every
reason to believe she would be. Who was the intruder? What was he,
or it, doing here? And what was he, or it, after? She shuddered at the

thought some ruthless thief might be planning to rob the place and there was nothing she could do about it. The river was between her and any sort of help.

She found no one and nothing unusual on the second floor, and on the third floor, even though she couldn't get at the rooms there, everything was quiet and appeared to be normal. She started to breathe a bit easier. She was approaching the landing to the attic when loud sounds, akin to chairs scraping against wooden floors, caused her to grip the railing anxiously.

As she reached the attic's parlor, loud thuds echoed from behind one of the locked doors, making her certain she was not alone in the mansion. Someone else was in the house. She took a deep breath and steeled herself for what might be an unpleasant confrontation. She thought it best to have some sort of weapon in her hand in case the unknown and unwanted visitor was hostile and had a weapon of his own.

With a growing sense of panic, she surveyed the small parlor. At the far end was a fireplace and, fortunately, there was an old fire poker leaning against the wooden pilaster that framed the fireplace. She went and took a firm hold of the poker, then marched toward the door from where the noise had emanated, her courage enhanced by the weapon clutched in her hand. As she called "Who's in there?" she also wrapped on the door with a tightly clenched fist.

The door opened so rapidly, she was taken off guard and raised the poker defensively. Her startled amber eyes widened at the sight before her.

CHAPTER 2

"Put that thing down before you hurt someone," the brawny giant thundered, looming over her as he slipped out the door and shut it behind him.

"Who are you? What are you doing here?" she demanded warily, lowering the poker to her side but still holding it tightly as the stranger's eyes seemed to devour her, sweeping over her with cool regard.

The man ignored her questions and walked past her to the observation deck. He put his hands on the railings to brace himself, surveying the scene as if he were king of the castle and everything in sight was his exclusive domain, which he ruled without question.

Anger swelled in Laura as she studied the back of this intruder with the eye of an artist. His large athletic form suggested a brute strength that could dominate any physical obstacles in its path and his wide shoulders only emphasized the narrowness of his hips. Instinctively Laura knew this was a man used to having his own way who would not tolerate interference from anyone. His clothes reminded her of the ones her father refused to part with but, somehow, her mother always managed to pilfer for rags—worn, patched, torn, stained and thoroughly out of date.

"Well . . . I asked you a question. Who are you?" she repeated irritably. "And what are you doing here?"

He turned and faced her, his steely blue eyes scanning her figure as if she were a prime steer up for auction. She flushed at the thought he was stripping her clothes off, one by one. But the impenetrable expression on his face gave her no clue as to what he was thinking. His inscrutable stare was becoming highly annoying and Laura felt herself on the verge of either screaming or lashing out at him physically.

"Listen, whoever you are, if you don't give me an explanation for your presence here, I'll let the authorities deal with you." Her eyes flashed and sparkled as her patience began to ebb.

His sardonic smile stressed the angular bones of his roughhewn face. "You're a short-tempered little wench, aren't you?"

"Only when I'm confronted with blatant rudeness, not to mention downright barbarous impudence. Most people I know are polite enough to answer a question when they are asked."

After some hesitation and a disdainful look in her direction, he finally spoke. "I'm Bert, the caretaker here. You don't think the owner would leave this place to the whimsies of vandals or thieves, do you?"

"I shouldn't think he would," Laura replied, her tension easing as she replaced the poker alongside the fireplace exactly as she had found it. "But it sounded to me as if you were making up for any damage vandals might do. Whatever happened up here? I could hear it all the way downstairs."

"I really don't think that is any of your business." His wide lips formed a grim line as he gazed at her suspiciously.

"I think it is. I was under the impression I was to be alone here."

"And I was under the impression they would send a man for such exacting work. Someone with experience instead of a green kid. And a girl at that!" he answered sarcastically.

"I'm not a green kid! My qualifications are of the highest. Not that you'd understand what the job entails. However, I am an expert at what I do whether you believe it or not," she retorted hotly. This rude, arrogant man was beginning to exasperate her beyond endurance.

"Are you now? A devoted career woman, I suppose," he sneered.

"And what is wrong with a woman having a career?" Laura asked, her small chin jutting out defiantly.

"Women should be at home, tending to a man and a family, not prancing about like some asexual peacock, flaunting authority and preening themselves for the next step up the ladder."

"Of all the narrow-minded . . . I think you've been on this island by yourself for too long. It's made you a bit lacking in the brain department, whatever-your-name is."

"Bert."

"The opportunities for women are just beginning to open up as the world realizes we have the same capabilities as any man," she continued with emphatic vehemence.

His rolling laughter was deep and sonorous but had a ring of mockery about it. "Do they now? I can think of several things a man can do that no woman can match. Shall I name them for you?"

There was a taunting derision in his steely eyes and the flush that was rising on her face was uncontrollable. "You know very well what I mean."

"Perhaps I do," he said more somberly. "But that doesn't alter my opinion of a woman's purpose in life. Quite honestly, I resent your intrusion on this island. Don't expect any welcome or assistance from me while you are here."

He turned to study the river again, frustrating Laura even further. She didn't like being dismissed out of hand. She headed for the stairs, trying to keep her temper in check. She was halfway down when she heard that deep, mellow voice of his call after her.

"What's your name?"

She turned to see his shadowy form towering above her at the top of the stairs. "Laura Bickford."

"Miss? Mrs.? or Ms.?"

"Miss Bickford will do nicely," she replied coolly.

"Well, Miss Bickford, I promise to stay out of your way if you'll promise to stay out of mine. They must have told you the third and fourth floors are off limits."

It was her turn to ignore him, she thought. But then, on impulse, she asked, "How did you know about me?"

"Mr. Harte told me there would be someone from the Brooklyn Museum to inventory the valuables on the first and second floors. By the way, you're not sleeping here, are you?"

"I have a motel room in town," she replied, thankful now that she did. The thought of spending even one night under the same roof as this overbearing brute horrified her. "I'll be leaving my equipment here though."

"Equipment?"

"Photographic equipment to take pictures of the articles I will be cataloging."

He stared at her long and hard. Laura felt her stomach roll in unknown fear. She raced down the stairs thinking what an insolent and barbarous man he was, no matter how handsome his facial features. She would be more than happy to comply with his wishes and stay completely out of his way.

As it was almost six o'clock, she picked up the satchel with the empty thermoses and her purse. She felt an odd uneasiness as she walked down the incline toward the dock. The very thought that he would be in the same house while she was working at the mansion unnerved her. She couldn't quite put her finger on what she found so profoundly disturbing about him, something in the way he looked at her. He was certainly puffed up with his own self-importance for a mere caretaker. She fervently hoped he would stay out of her way and sight for the duration of her stay on the isolated island. She could only take him in little doses. To have to spend large blocks of time with him would leave her so flustered, it would make it difficult to concentrate on the work she came to do.

Off in the distance she spied the boat heading toward the island and an inordinate sense of relief swept through her. A feeling of elation replaced the uncomfortable emotions that had been plaguing her as Kevin's handsome face came into view.

"Well, how did it go?" he shouted as the boat slid in beside the dock.

"Quite well, considering."

Kevin extended his hand, which Laura grasped as she jumped into the swaying boat. "Considering what?" he asked.

"Considering the impossible caretaker there."

"Oh, him. Don't let him bother you. He seems like a nice enough fellow. Anyway, he's harmless enough, even though he can display a wicked temper at times. I'm sure he'll leave you to your own devices. Not much of a mixer."

She was about to reply when the roar of the engine not only drowned out her voice but also her thoughts.

Laura collapsed on the bed in the motel room, her mind whirling between the grandeur of the mansion and the crudeness of its caretaker. She was on the verge of drowsing off when Kevin's parting words rang like an alarm bell in her head. "I'll pick you up at seven-thirty."

With an extreme exertion of willpower, she rose and got into a steamy shower. She slipped into a pale yellow dress whose tight bodice and billowy skirt complemented her youthful figure. Looking in the mirror, she recalled those cold, blue eyes of the caretaker assessing her so knowingly. She shook her head clear of the apparition and put on matching shoes. The pale yellow pocketbook completed the outfit and created an air of delicate perfection. Kevin pulled into the courtyard of the motel minutes after Laura had seated herself in one of the lounging chairs outside.

"Been waiting long?" he asked, smiling with that boyish grin of his that Laura found most engaging.

"No," she answered as she went to the car and got in.

"There's a nice little restaurant about three miles out of town. Do you mind the drive?"

"On the contrary. When someone else is driving, I find it refreshing. Besides, after the mileage I put on yesterday, three miles seems like a short hop."

"Do you like haute cuisine?"

"Out here? Don't tell me you have restaurants that cater to gourmet taste buds?" She smiled and arched her eyebrows quizzically.

Kevin laughed and looked at her fleetingly. "Is that so unusual? You forget that a lot of wealthy people have homes here in the Thousand Islands and we also have our fair share of tourists. Consequently, the restaurant does quite well. Then too, the food is excellent, as you shall soon see." There were several moments of silence before Kevin continued. "Did you accomplish anything at the mansion today?"

"More than I thought I would, in spite of the altercation with the caretaker. Tomorrow I'll bring the stands and tripods—then I can really get to work and get some photographs taken. Oh, before I forget, nine o'clock tomorrow?"

"Yes, ma'am."

It seemed to Laura she had just settled down in comfort when they arrived at the restaurant on the outskirts of town.

It was a small, cozy place. The tables were tastefully set, almost touching on elegance. Kevin was greeted warmly. It was obvious he was a frequent and well-known patron. When the waiter brought the menu, Kevin waved it away, saying, "Have Henri choose our meal. He knows what is best today." The waiter nodded in smiling approval. "And bring us a bottle of Puligny-Montrachet '70," he added confidently.

Again the waiter nodded before disappearing into the kitchen. In less than five minutes he emerged with a bottle of wine nestled in a bed of ice on a rolling chrome cart, the latter also bearing their appetizers.

"Well, Mr. Courtney, I'm duly impressed," stated Laura.

"Kevin. Please. I wanted to show you we are not backward here." His hazel eyes gazed at her with a beguiling charm and his smile could almost have been termed seductive. Laura cautioned herself about being lured into another situation like the one with Peter.

"I didn't mean to imply that. It's only . . . well . . . I feel like I've been transported to Quo Vadis—a very posh restaurant in New York City."

"The food is comparable but not the prices."

"You're familiar with the city?"

"I was born there."

Amazement was clearly etched on Laura's smooth face as she swirled the succulent bits of shrimp, crabmeat and lobster in the horseradish-tomato sauce before plopping them into her mouth, piece by tender piece.

"I've surprised you, haven't I?" Kevin asked as he savored the bits of crustaceans.

"Yes, you did. But then, when a countrified Vermonter moves to the big city and submits to immediate absorption, they tend to think of everyone else as provincial except themselves. How long were you there?"

"Until I graduated from New York University at the age of twenty-two."

"How did you ever end up here?"

"Came up to see the Clayton Boat Museum for a paper I was working on and liked the area so much that when I graduated I moved up here."

"No regrets?"

"None at all. And you? Are you happy in your work?"

Laura smiled. "More than I thought possible."

"Doesn't it get tedious writing down descriptions of things all day long?"

"Some objects are not at all easy to describe. They can present quite a challenge. And photographing the object to its best advantage can be difficult at times."

"Sounds more interesting, and more complicated, than I thought it would be. Living in the city, social life must also take a heavy toll on your time."

Laura did not want to discuss her private life with a man who was almost a stranger to her. She was spared the effort of a reply when the waiter cleared the table and placed bowls of clear, hot mushroom soup before them. She could feel Kevin's eyes on her as they consumed the delicious soup. He was a good-looking, pleasant man and she would like to be friends with him but nothing more. No more deep emotional involvements. She would allow herself this social interlude with Kevin, for she knew as soon as her assignment was over she would never see him again. Six weeks wasn't enough time to become seriously entangled with anyone, at least, not enough for her.

"A penny for your thoughts," said Kevin softly.

"That would be a gross overpayment indeed."

"You seemed so far away."

"Not really. Just making some mental notes for tomorrow's work," she fibbed.

"I'm crushed. How can you think about work when you're with me?" he chided her playfully.

"You're right. I'm being rude. I promise not to let my work enter my mind for the rest of the evening. If you don't mind, I would like to know what kind of boats you build. I've never met someone who builds boats from scratch."

When the waiter came to remove the empty soup bowls, Kevin ordered another bottle of wine, then proceeded to give her a detailed

steep incline. One of the tripods escaped her grasp and went clatter-
ing down the hill. An insolent laugh pierced the still air. Laura
turned and looked up to see the satanic face of the caretaker watching her with joyous mirth, his thick black hair ruffling in the breeze
as he stood majestically on the deck.

"It's not funny," she shouted resentfully.

"All women are funny," he retorted coolly, all laughter erased by
a sudden somber mood.

Laura seethed inside. Her opinion of men, most men anyway, was
reinforced by the surly example standing above her on the attic balcony. She stormed into the house and put her equipment down when
she reached the library. She sat down heavily in the chair still smoldering at being an object for his derision. By a caretaker, no less!
Who did he think he was? Now she could think of a thousand witty
replies to his rudeness. But then, it had always been that way with
her. Whenever she was confronted with unpleasantness, she would
walk off, speechless. Only on reflection could she think of clever
remarks to offset her adversary.

"Well, I'd better go get that tripod and get to work," she sighed
aloud to the empty library.

It was after lunch. Laura had set up the lights and camera in the
reception room, with the camera focused on William Chadwick's
painting "On the Porch." She found the mansion to be a treasure-
house of early American Impressionism paintings. This was Laura's
element and she reveled in it.

She had taken one picture of it and was about to take another for
good measure when she heard the front door open and the heavy
pod of feet on the marble entry floor.

She had kept her promise and stayed out of the caretaker's way,
now why couldn't he keep his and stay out of hers?

"Hello there! Anybody here?" The voice was that of a woman.

Brimming with curiosity, Laura opened the door and looked into
the foyer.

"There you are. I've been looking forward to meeting you. I'm
Hannah Lawson, your next-door neighbor so to speak. I hope I'm
not disturbing you," said the formidable, sixtyish woman who firmly
strode toward Laura with a regal air and her hand extended in
greeting.

"How do you do. I'm—"

"I know who you are, Miss Bickford. Even though we may live
isolated on islands we all know what is going on in every one of
them. At least those in our immediate vicinity. Do you have any

account of the various types of boats he was commissioned t[...] Laura listened with interest until the waiter brought the main [...] A murmur of awe escaped her lips.

"Ah, *caneton à l'orange*. Henri's specialty of the house. He [...] eye of a true artist when it comes to preparing food. It is as a[...] to the eye as it is to the palate."

Laura agreed as the juices of appetite formed in her mou[...] moned by the tempting aroma of the hot duckling.

It was quite late when Kevin turned the car into the mo[...] yard. Laura's head was floating with more wine than she w[...] tomed to but not enough to affect her decision regarding [...] tional involvement with a man. As Kevin shut off the ig[...] turned to her, she sprang out of the car, profusely thanki[...] the marvelous dinner and telling him she would see him [...] the marina. He called to her but she rushed into her mote[...] fore his words could reach her.

The next day dawned crisp and clear. A cool shower [...] walk to the restaurant in the fresh air removed the sli[...] headache Laura had awakened with. Too much wine, [...] After a hearty breakfast, she lugged the tripods and sta[...] the marina expecting to see Kevin waiting for her with [...] smile and friendly greeting. Even though his boat was s[...] side, the dock was empty. There was no Kevin to rush t[...] relieve her of some of her burdens.

"Kevin?" she called several times to no avail. It see[...] boat was deserted. She began to wonder if he had ta[...] her abrupt departure last night. Maybe she had been [...] had appeared discourteous. Her mind shifted to alte[...] reaching the island when a craggy, weatherworn face [...] the small cabin.

"Was havin' a bit of a nap, miss. But I'm ready t[...] the bent figure emerging from the cabin.

"Where is Mr. Courtney?" she asked.

"Oh, he had to go to Montreal. Business. Asked [...] over to the mansion."

Laura was disappointed. She had wanted to mak[...] her swift departure last night and thank him once ag[...] evening.

The grizzled old man steered the boat through t[...] with obvious skill. He whipped it alongside the i[...] careless ease. She thanked him and with ladened [...] the dock.

It was awkward carrying the odd-shaped stands [...]

tea?" Hannah asked, finally releasing Laura's hand from her strong grasp.

"I have a thermos of coffee left," answered Laura, bewildered yet amused by this intrusion.

"Never touch it. Horrible stuff. Well, what do you think of Evans Mansion, girl?"

"I find it extremely fascinating, Mrs. Lawson."

"It's 'miss.' But call me Hannah. Can't abide silly formalities. I don't have that much time to waste at my age. If I like someone, I skip all the folderol and get to basics."

"And how can you be sure you'll like me? You don't even know me," Laura questioned, an amused smile on her lips.

"I saw you land the other day with such firmness of purpose that, at first, I thought you might be a bit stuffy and a righteous prude, even though you are such a pretty child. But when I saw you drop that piece of iron this morning, I knew you were vulnerable just like the rest of us."

"You must have very keen eyesight."

"No. Very strong binoculars. Have you had lunch?"

"Yes."

"Too bad. Perhaps I can cook for you another day. I'm an excellent chef, if I do say so myself. Don't eat your lunch before one o'clock. If I'm coming, it will be before then. Well now, have you seen the grounds?"

"Not really. Only what I could see from the main path."

"Then you've missed half the mansion," declared Hannah Lawson, her eyebrows arched imperiously over deep blue eyes.

"Perhaps when I'm through with my work, I'll take a stroll around the island."

"Nonsense. No time like the present. Put on your sweater and come tromp around the place with me. It'll do your bones good . . . and your spirit. I always make it a point to have a good bracing walk after lunch. It stimulates the digestive juices."

"The caretaker here might disapprove of our trespassing on the grounds," suggested Laura, recalling his churlish manner.

"Bert? Why should he?"

"He seems very protective about this place."

"He should be. That's what he gets paid for." Hannah's stern face softened. "By George, if I were thirty years younger, I'd set my cap for that man. He's so handsome in a devilish way and with a physique to match. A real man's man." Hannah sighed deeply.

"Too bad his temper isn't as appealing," Laura stated with disdain.

"I gather you've met him."

"Encounter would be a better word. Is he from around here?"

"No. Not originally. About seven or eight years ago he started spending the summers here. Became somewhat of a warm weather fixture."

"What did he do before he became the caretaker of Evans Mansion?"

"General handyman. He worked on some of the dairy farms, then worked for Kevin Courtney for a spell last year. I have the impression he's one of those itinerant workers. You know the sort. They work their way north in the summer and south in the winter. I take it you don't care for the man."

"I find him arrogant and ill-mannered. And he makes his antipathy to women more than evident."

"You may be right there. In all the years he's been coming here, I've never seen him with a woman and there was never any talk in town about his womanizing. Not that I haven't heard some of the women talking about him. And in very flattering tones. Oh, well, enough said on that subject. Come along."

Laura felt there was no denying Hannah Lawson. She was the kind of person who, having an objective in mind, would let nothing deter her, not even a division of heavily armed troops. She obediently followed the older woman outside. Instinctively Laura looked up at the attic balcony, half expecting to find the caretaker looking down at her with a chilling sneer on his thin, sensuous lips. But there was no one there.

Laura had to quicken her pace to keep up with Hannah Lawson's martial stride.

"Look ahead, my girl. Can you see it?" asked Hannah, who managed to nod her head with her chin held high.

Laura peered at a square stone building that resembled a Greek temple. "What is it? Another house?"

"In a way. Can you imagine that beautiful edifice houses steam generators? Evans intended to electrify the entire island. Coal was brought by barges up the river to fire the generators and underground cables were laid leading into the house."

"So that's where the electricity comes from. I was wondering because I hadn't seen any outside wires."

"The generators that lie behind that archaic facade have been dormant for many a year now. I believe what electricity there is in the house now comes from a small generator in the basement of the mansion. It generates enough power to provide some of the necessities on the first floor. The rest of the floors have outlets but no power, last I heard. I understand the new owner, Nathaniel Harte, is going to try and use the flow of the river to turn the generators. I wish him luck. This river has a whimsy of its own."

Laura followed Hannah around the island, the silence broken only by Hannah's remarks on the various vistas seen on the river.

"There, girl! Feast your eyes on that!"

"What in heaven's name is it?" asked Laura, amazed at the sight. It seemed to hang over the river like a shadowy castle. It was an enormous building graced with miniature turrets and doors so huge and heavy an engine was required to open and close them.

"The yacht house, child, the yacht house. Why, in my day, yachts with tall masts and their rigging still standing sailed right in. An awesome sight, believe me. It is a marvelous structure, don't you think?"

"Impressive to say the least," admitted Laura.

"I remember Gerald Evans at the helm steering one of his larger yachts right into the bowels of the thing. He was a handsome devil."

"You knew Mr. Evans?"

"Oh, yes. We attended many of the balls held here. He had a magnetic charm women found hard to resist, much like your caretaker."

"He's not *my* caretaker. Heaven forbid!" Then after a slight pause, "If you'll forgive my brashness, Miss Lawson—"

"Hannah."

"Hannah. It sounds like you were almost in love with Mr. Evans," observed Laura as they slowly turned in the direction of the dock.

"Almost in love? Why, girl, it was a grand passion. Sorry to say, only on my part. I was but a slip of a girl, if you can imagine that, and he was the older married man, which, incidentally, made him all the more desirable in my eyes. Ah, but that is a story to be told over a cup of tea. My yacht awaits!" She waved nonchalantly toward a small rowboat bobbing next to the dock. "I shall return. Didn't someone else say that once? Well, no matter. We must have lunch and get to know each other better. I think I'm going to like you very much, Laura Bickford. Yes. I like the ring of that. Laura Bickford," she repeated. She gave a quick approving nod of her head as though she had made some inner decision.

With firm, steady strokes, Hannah rowed away toward a small island directly across from the dock while Laura waved good-bye vigorously.

On the way back to the mansion, Laura found herself intrigued by this stately woman who, evidently, lived all alone on an island in the middle of the river. She wondered why. For Hannah Lawson was certainly a pleasant, gregarious person and Laura genuinely liked her in spite of her overbearing airs.

She entered the library and was staggered to find the huge hulk of the caretaker seated at her desk and reading her catalog descriptions. Engrossed, he didn't notice her presence. She observed the tranquil look on his face that heightened his rugged good looks and gave him a deep aura of sensitivity. She was about to make an attempt at friendliness when he looked up. His brows knitted together in a frown at the sight of her.

"I see you've been trotting all over the grounds. Have you nothing better to do? I wasn't aware you were here to sight-see."

His eyes assessed her slim figure with an audacity that made Laura uncomfortable. Her body stiffened instantly.

"And have you nothing better to do than to poke into other people's private matters?"

He stood with a suddenness that made the chair scrape the floor roughly. "I wasn't aware these papers were for your eyes only." He leaned forward, his clenched fists firmly braced on the desk. "It is my duty to know everything about this place and what goes on here. It is under my care."

"I'm not under your care and neither is my work. I'll thank you to leave."

Bert came from behind the desk to confront her at closer range. He glared down at her, his voice husky as he muttered, "Young girls like you should be under someone's care. Running about unattended, you're liable to do harm, not only to those around you but to yourself."

Laura shivered nervously. His physical proximity was causing her to lose her composure and that was the last thing she wanted to do in front of him.

"And there are some men who shouldn't be left to wander about unattended," she retorted defiantly, adding, "Whatever happened to your pledge to stay out of my way?"

A cynical smile played around the corners of his mouth but his darkened blue eyes blazed at her with fiery indignation. "No woman dictates to me. I'll go where I please, when I please."

"It was your choice." Laura felt victorious when she saw his hands whiten at the knuckles as his fists doubled even tighter. But the feeling of victory soon dissipated as he stepped closer and his enigmatic smile widened.

"You mean if it were your choice you would have preferred my company?" There was a peculiar warmth in his eyes that betrayed a sensitivity and kindness lurking in the depths beyond his gruff exterior.

Laura stepped backwards, bumping into one of her lighting fixtures, which in turn toppled with a resounding thud as she landed on her rump unceremoniously.

He rushed to her side offering his hand as his expression clouded with concern. "Are you all right?"

"I . . . I think so," she stammered, knowing her face was flushing red at her own clumsiness.

His strong hand closed over hers and helped her to her feet with a gentleness that startled her. A lean finger tilted her chin up, forcing her eyes to meet his. "No broken bones?" he asked softly.

"I don't think so," she replied, letting a smile creep across her oval face as she studied his clear blue eyes. There was something about the man that haunted her. It was as if he was trying to mask a vulnerability under a guise of churlishness. Maybe her initial reaction to him had been misguided and she should be more tolerant. After all, she really knew nothing about him and it was always a mistake to make snap judgments.

His eyes bore into hers for a moment longer before he stooped to put her light back in place.

"Thank you," she murmured.

"Do I frighten you, Miss Bickford?" he asked, using one of his lean fingers to brush aside a stray tendril of her honey-blond hair.

"No," she replied a little too quickly, as if she was trying to hide a truth she didn't want to admit.

"You'll have to realize I didn't expect to have such a lovely young girl on this island. I'll have to confess it's thrown me off guard. Unexpected disruptions have a way of bringing out the worst in me. I'll try to keep the unruly part of my nature in check while you grace this humble island."

"I would consider it most gracious of you if you did."

"Never let it be said I was ungracious, especially to a young lady. I hope you will reward my endeavor by not snooping about the place other than the two floors assigned to you."

"I won't have time to 'snoop about,' as you put it. I have far too much work to do to be sidetracked by nonessential curiosity," she stated flatly.

He ran his fingers carelessly through his thick black hair, a latent whimsy in his eyes. "I wish I could say as much."

"What do you mean?"

"Nothing, Miss Bickford, nothing at all." He paused, his gaze skimming over her wantonly. "Tell me, do you have a steady boy-friend?"

"I don't think that is any of your business," she retorted testily. Her personal life was none of his concern and she thought it rude of him to even ask such a question.

He shrugged indifferently. "I find it hard to understand why some man hasn't scooped you up before this. Or does your career take precedence over all else?"

"My career is only one facet of my life . . . one I enjoy very much . . . but I don't let it dominate my every waking moment." He was being far too inquisitive and it was making her uneasy. "Now if you'll excuse me, I have work to do." Laura was proud of her ability to act calm and civil in spite of the turmoil he caused within her.

She walked past him haughtily, her shoulder brushing against his broad chest and sending a small tremor crackling down her spine.

"Never let it be said I came between a woman and her work." He gave a shallow, mocking bow and left the room. She could hear the sound of his feet as he climbed the marble steps in the hall, presumably on his way to his quarters in the attic.

Her hands trembled as she slid into the chair so recently vacated by the caretaker; its warmth wending its way into her body and filling her with a mixture of anger and uncertainty. The insufferable boor, she thought. As she studied the next item to be cataloged, a disquietude kept infringing on her train of thought. Why couldn't they have hired some nice old man as a caretaker? Why this big argumentative brute of a man that seemed to have the knack of reaching into her soul and turning it inside out. His attractive masculinity had a way of intruding on her efforts to concentrate on the work at hand.

With a deliberate, conscious straining of her willpower, she managed to focus her attention on the papers before her, but she found even the tiniest noise would send her blood racing. She didn't know if it was annoyance or dread she felt but she did know a glowing heat filled her at the sight of him. She knew her heart would pound erratically at the mere thought of the caretaker entering the room again.

The next several days passed uneventfully. Laura was a bit perplexed by the absence of Hannah Lawson, for the woman had seemed so friendly at first. Her thoughts about Kevin Courtney were a little more disconcerting. He had seemingly vanished from Alexandria Bay and his substitute didn't have any answers about Kevin's whereabouts when Laura questioned him. She was torn between concern for his well-being and a regret for her abrupt dismissal of him the night he had taken her to dinner. He hadn't made any passes at her nor did he give any indication he would. Yet she had fled from him as if he were some wild beast about to attack her. Overreaction to snap judgments was a trait she would have to take in hand and cure. Kevin appeared to have all the characteristics of a gentleman.

She was not so sure about Bert, the caretaker. At times the latter seemed to have all the makings of a penned up wild animal. Yet, underlying any feral instincts, he appeared to possess a deep compassionate nature. Inherently, she knew when this man loved it would not be capriciously. He would love with a strong conviction that would underline the words "till death do us part." Her heart tripped a little at the thought of being loved by such a man and a delightful shudder raced through her to think of what he would do if his primitive energies were ever let loose.

She knew she shouldn't let her imagination run wild in a tantalizing daydream, but she had a premonition that this caretaker was everything Peter wasn't. There was something about him that precluded his using people to gratify his male ego, and if he ever made an emotional commitment it would be for eternity. She sighed and smiled at her own foolish mental wanderings. She was there to do a job and not to become a simpering romantic over a man she had just met. Besides, even though the scars from her interlude with Peter had healed, she was still cautious about letting her emotions hold sway over her common sense. No matter how she yearned to be in love and have the right man love her, she wasn't about to dive into a restless sea blindfolded and without a life preserver.

A silly giggle bounced through her head as she wondered what her girl friends back in Brooklyn would think if they knew she was alone on an island with an extremely handsome caretaker. They'd probably think she was crazy not to take advantage of the situation by yielding to her romantic nature. They certainly would, especially Isabel. She could picture Isabel fluttering her long eyelashes and flirting outrageously as she tried to appear seductive and glamorous. But her efforts only succeeded in being comically cute, which most men found endearing anyway.

Laura often wished she could toss her inhibitions to the wind and be like Isabel, so extroverted and, at times, positively reckless. Maybe someday I will, but I have plenty of time for that, she thought idly.

CHAPTER 3

Every morning like clockwork, Laura gingerly hopped from the boat and, in a springing gait, satchel and purse rhythmically swaying, strode up the path to the mansion, her honey-gold hair sparkling as the sun caught its bouncing flow. The work fascinated and delighted her. In fact it didn't seem like work at all, more like a vacation, studying and handling those items she adored. So captivated by the mansion and its contents, she went around the gracious house with a look of vulnerable femininity. She never noticed the steely blue eyes that watched her every movement with a peculiar wistfulness as they gazed furtively from the house and from the attic window as she approached every morning. She had recaptured her former sense of dedication and was so absorbed in the tasks at hand she had forgotten about Kevin and the caretaker.

She released a long, low, audible sigh as she sat behind the mahogany desk and surveyed her notes with a smile of self-satisfaction. With lips pursed, she rose from the desk and snapped on the bright floodlights that were aimed at a painting on one of the tripods. Her lithe body moved with agility from light to light, adjusting and readjusting, until she thought the picture was illuminated to the best possible advantage. Having secured what she knew would be a good shot of the painting, she lifted it off the easel. Her work was going better than she had expected. In another week or so, she would have photographed and cataloged all the contents of the first floor and could commence her work on the second.

She looked at the green drop cloth she had used as a background for the painting and decided she needn't leave it up there any longer, for she had done all the paintings downstairs. As she pulled it down, revealing the bookcases behind it, a large volume caught her eye. It was bound in green leather with the word *Remington* stamped in gold on the spine.

She took it from the shelf, placed it on the desk and opened it to the first page. The name in bold type, on the flyleaf, was Frederic Sackrider Remington. It was a biography of the great artist, noted for his Western paintings and illustrations, along with a huge pictorial supplement of his works including a number of his pencil sketches. It was an answer to her prayers. The nights in her motel room were an exercise in loneliness and boredom. Television offered nothing but uninteresting repeats of shows that had been dull in the first place. She had read the books she had brought with her and was about to take up knitting. This book on Remington would go a long way to brighten her evenings at the motel. She slipped it into the satchel she would be taking back to the mainland with her.

Once on shore, Laura stopped in the town's small variety store and purchased a low-priced transistor radio, then grabbed a bite to eat before heading back to the motel. She thought some light music in the background would help dispel the eerie stillness that pervaded the mansion. A little music always aided her as she photographed and she could listen to it in the motel room instead of the drone of the television.

She entered the motel room, content with her purchase and looking forward to perusing the Remington book. She took a hot shower, then curled up on the bed with the book. It wasn't long before she fell into a dreamless sleep.

The morning dawned gray, slate-colored clouds obscuring the sun. There was a mist in the air as she trod the now familiar streets to the restaurant. She was carefully placing pats of butter between her pancakes when a voice intruded on her solitude.

"Miss me?"

She looked up to see the sparkling hazel eyes and wind-blown sandy hair of Kevin Courtney.

"Kevin!" Her voice betrayed her genuine delight in seeing him. "How was Montreal?"

"Lucrative. A commission to design and build a forty-six-foot yacht. Not bad for a little over a week's work." He smiled and it was infectious.

"I should say not. Was it difficult to obtain the contract?"

"Not at all. I had the contract the second day I was there."

"I hear Montreal is an interesting city with some splendid old churches and shops," she commented, wondering what took him so long if he had the contract in two days. She quickly chided herself for her curiosity. It was really none of her business what Kevin did.

"I suppose it is. All I saw this time were the restaurants and night spots. My customer insisted I get to know her personality, her likes and dislikes, so I could incorporate all this fascinating knowledge into the design of her yacht."

"Her? Funny, I never thought of women having yachts commissioned. I always thought it was strictly a male-oriented business."

"Believe it or not, a great many of my clients are women, the little treasures. They pay handsomely to get precisely what they want. The men are tighter with the purse strings, so I naturally prefer the ladies."

"Anyone in particular?"

"Good Lord! No! Never. I enjoy playing the field. If a relationship veers toward the serious I become the invisible man and duck out faster than a laser beam. I have no intention of ever becoming tied down with one woman." He glanced at her with impish amusement. "I hope I haven't disillusioned you."

"No. Not at all. I appreciate your honesty. At least a girl knows where she stands with you," replied Laura, a bit startled by his declaration.

"She sure does. However, I don't exactly love them and leave them. I make quite sure they know from the very beginning that I'm not the marrying kind. But never mind me, how are you coming at the mansion? Still hard at work?"

"Everything is going along as scheduled, even better," she answered, a certain reserve slipping back into her voice. "I've almost finished the first floor and my job will be done when I've completed the second."

"You're moving right along then. What a pity! Couldn't you slow it up a bit?"

"Whatever for?" Laura's finely arched eyebrows lifted at the suggestion.

"So we could have more time to become better acquainted."

Blushing at his implication, Laura looked at her watch in an attempt to hide her embarrassment. "It's after nine. I'm running late today. Are you taking me to the island?"

"Of course. I wouldn't dream of missing an opportunity to be with so lovely a creature as you, even though it appears I run out on you at the slightest provocation. Besides, I want to make sure you get back safe and sound so I can take you to dinner and the dance in town tonight. I think you will enjoy it. Nothing but old-time music from our very own sentimental orchestra. Not always in tune but they try hard."

His handsome weathered face was eager and Laura didn't have the heart to refuse him. Besides, she thought, some wholesome socializing would do her a world of good and renew her spirits.

On the island, Laura hummed along when the small radio played a familiar tune and tackled her work with joyous abandon. The thought of not having to sit all alone in the motel room lightened her mood. It had been a long time since she had gone dancing and she was eagerly looking forward to it.

The music swarmed around her in muted tones, imbuing her with a gaiety she hadn't felt for some time. But it came to a crashing halt when the radio was abruptly snapped off. She spun the swivel chair around to find the cause of the sudden silence.

"Are you trying to arouse the dead with that infernal noise?" The angry caretaker glared down at her, his eyes daring her to speak.

"It isn't noise. It's music. And what gives you the right to come bursting in here and tell me what I can or cannot do?" She got up from the chair and went to the radio, defiantly turning it back on.

Like a raging bull, he stormed to her side, grasped the radio, once again shutting it off, and held it high over his head.

"Please don't," cried Laura, her innocent eyes beseeching him not to hurl the delicate instrument to the floor.

"Why not?" he asked as a taunting smile formed on his lips.

Her eyes were glued to the small radio, which seemed to be on the verge of being hurled into space. In vain her arms struggled to retrieve it as he held it aloft just out of her reach, watching her take small leaps toward it.

"Do you seriously think you can take it from me if I don't want you to have it?" The derisive humor in his eyes infuriated her.

"You have no right to touch my property," she growled through clenched teeth, then made a bounding jump for his upstretched arm, only to lose her balance and crash against him.

His free arm swept around her small waist and caught her from stumbling to the floor. She gaped at him in total surprise to find all the humor had left his craggy face. His arm tightened like a steel band drawing her slim body against his well-muscled form. Mesmerized by the intent look in his eyes and the unexpected turn of events, she offered no resistance as she stared in bewilderment at the face that was lowering slowly to meet hers.

Suddenly realizing what was happening, she opened her mouth to protest only to have him effectively silence her as his lips coaxed her own to respond. His lips moved over hers with a fiery tenderness, causing her legs to feel like wet paper bags, unable to support her. She knew she had made a mistake letting herself yield even a bit but it was too late to rescind as the all-consuming madness devoured her. He had an irresistible power over her and she felt helpless, unable to fight the demands of his searing kiss. Somewhere along the way, he had replaced the small radio on the stand and both arms now en-

circled her with crushing precision while his fierce kiss excited her
senses with its insolent possession and forceful urgency.

Sanity returning, she couldn't and wouldn't let him dominate her.
The hypnotic effect had to be broken. She drew her arms up against
his wide chest and began to push with all the strength she could command as her head twisted from side to side trying to wrench her lips
free of his.

Expecting a life and death struggle to extricate herself from his
hold, she was startled when he instantly released her. She couldn't
bring herself to look at him and rushed to the front of the desk, taking small gasps of air as she placed her hands flat out on the top of
the shiny mahogany desk to steady her trembling body. When a measure of composure returned, she swung around to face him.

"What kind of animal are you to take advantage of my isolation
here?" Her voice quavered.

"The kind of animal that quickly responds when a beautiful young
woman throws herself at him," he responded, his eyes like molten
steel as they raked her face with blatant adoration and desire.

"I did not throw myself at you!" she protested.

"Didn't you? I seem to recall a warm body being cast into my
arms."

"You know damn well I lost my balance and couldn't help it," she
fumed.

He shrugged, seemingly disinterested. "You are free to make
whatever excuses you like." He turned his back to her and walked to
the window, where he drew the curtains back with one hand, then
leaned against the frame.

"Is this little episode indicative of what I might expect for the re-
mainder of my stay on this island?" she asked with a calmness she
didn't know she possessed.

"I deeply regret the incident and I assure you it won't happen
again unless, of course, you provoke me." He continued to stare out
the window, his powerful frame silhouetted against the light.

"I provoke you? Of all the nerve! You are the most . . . most
. . . most arrogant man I've ever met." Her voice was becoming
strident but she didn't care. Who did he think he was . . . this . . .
this . . . caretaker? She didn't have the time to indulge in fanciful
battles with him. She had work to do and it had to be completed in
an allotted amount of time, and do it she would, in spite of him. It
was the first assignment in which she was completely on her own and
she desperately wanted to do a good job. It would be a feather in her
cap that might possibly lead to bigger and more complicated assign-

ments. She wasn't about to jeopardize her career for some egotistical caretaker. "If you don't mind I have work to do."

"I don't mind. Please continue."

"Your presence here is distracting to say the least."

"Thank you."

"Don't flatter yourself. I've always found it difficult to concentrate when there is a strange presence in the room. A dog or a cat would be just as distracting."

There was a cynical smile on his face when he finally turned to face her. "I trust the matter of the radio is settled?"

"I'll keep it low," she compromised.

"See that you do." He thrust his hands in the pockets of his sloppy, stained khaki pants and started toward the door, where he stopped abruptly.

"By the way, take it easy with the lights. Don't use them unnecessarily, I don't think the generator can take it."

Before she could reply, he had gone.

Kevin's lighthearted banter kept her mind occupied on the ride back to the mainland. But alone in the motel, a shudder convulsed her as she recalled the passionate, probing kiss that had taken her unaware, and what disturbed her even more was the fact she had begun to respond in kind. When his arm went around her and the heat of his body flowed into hers, a tingle had started in her toes, increasing in intensity as it coursed upward and dispersed itself throughout her entire being. No man had ever made her experience a throbbing arousal like that. Not even Peter. It frightened and allured her at the same time.

She glanced at her watch and jumped up from the bed, alarmed that her musings had made her forget all about the time. She would have to hurry if she was to be ready when Kevin called for her.

Now she was glad she had packed the emerald-green chiffon dress. She had brought it with her on a whim, never thinking she would really have the opportunity to wear it. It was a wisp of a dress. Thin shoulder straps holding the low-cut bodice, which clung to her upper form before it billowed into yards of filmy chiffon swirling down to an ankle-length skirt. The open-toed, spaghetti-strapped shoes had been dyed to match. It was one of her rare extravagances.

She luxuriated under the hot beads of water bursting from the shower head while working mounds of foamy suds into her hair. After a brisk rubdown with the towel, she started to dress. All her hair needed was some brushing and it would be dry. She slipped into her dress, applied some perfume and light makeup and was ready. She glanced quickly into the mirror and was pleased with the reflection. Impatiently she looked forward to an evening away from the dismal confines of her motel room. She was even beginning to have pangs of homesickness and longed to be back in her apartment and among her friends. The itinerant life was not for her, she decided. Especially when one was alone.

Kevin took her to the same restaurant where, once again, he displayed his knowledge of wines and food and where Henri outdid himself in a choice of menu for them. She never realized how tasty lamb could be until Henri made it for them with his usual culinary skill.

Fully sated, Laura leaned back in the car seat and closed her eyes, a faint smile on her lips.

"Tired?" Kevin asked.

"Not really. Just content. The dinner was absolutely delicious and I want to thank you."

"It is I who must thank you for letting me enjoy the company of so beautiful a young woman."

"My, you are gallant tonight."

"Only being honest." He paused thoughtfully, then continued, "Is there something wrong, Laura? You have a strange look about you. Has Bert been giving you any trouble out there?"

"No trouble really. It's his attitude I find irritating," she replied, trying to keep her thoughts from dwelling on the kiss he had given her.

Kevin shrugged. "I'll have to admit he's an odd duck. But don't let him get you down. As I said before, I think he's harmless enough. More bark than bite if you know what I mean."

"Well, we pretty much steer clear of each other. It seems we can't have a civilized conversation. It always ends up in an argument. I do my best to avoid him and he reciprocates, which suits me just fine."

"That would be the last thing I'd be doing if I were in his place." His eyes twinkled with a devilish glint.

"What do you mean?"

"I wouldn't let you out of my sight for one minute. I'd make up the silliest excuses to be close to you." He glanced at her admiringly.

"Are we almost there?" she asked, hoping to change the subject.

"Don't want to talk about it, do you? It's okay. I can wait," he said with good humor as he turned the car into a long driveway leading to a large white Victorian inn.

"Is this where the dance is?"

"Surprised?"

"Yes. I am."

Kevin parked the car and led her to the broad marble steps leading to the main entrance of the inn.

The setting of the dance was not what Laura had expected. For some reason, she had envisioned a rustic barn decorated with paper lanterns. Instead, she was entering a vast ballroom located on the first floor of the turn-of-the-century hotel, complete with marble floor and crystal chandelier. It was similar to the one at Evans Mansion, except for the numerous small tables and chairs around the spacious room. At the far end was a small stage where the orchestra was seated. The musicians were formally attired in white tie and tails. It was a scene from the past, needing only the wide flowing ball gowns of the last century to complete it. But that was not the case. The majority of the people were dressed in modern clothes and some of them were a little on the extreme side.

A stiff-backed waiter, sporting a moustache, escorted them to one of the round tables whose candle flickered like a rainbow in its multicolored glass holder.

"You still have that look of awe on your face. What did you expect?" Kevin asked after ordering the wine.

"Something a little homier, I guess. Certainly nothing like this."

Kevin laughed. "I'll admit we are a bit rural but we're not aborigines, you know. We have all the latest innovations and are thoroughly modernized. Why, we even have television out here," he teased. "But I guess we do tend to cling to some of the finer niceties of a bygone era."

"This ballroom certainly gives evidence to that. It is truly charming."

"They hold a number of dances here. More frequently in the winter. And they do cater to the older crowd with music from the past. The younger people have their own bands, or should I call them groups? A little too loud for my tastes, though. I had a feeling you would enjoy this more than the disco sound. I hope I wasn't wrong."

"No. Not at all. I enjoy watching disco dancers if the dancers are exceptionally good. But enough is enough. I really prefer the slower, more tuneful music."

"Shall we dance?" asked Kevin as the violins started to play a melodic fox-trot.

"By all means."

Kevin held her close as the string section seductively played an old love song. She could feel the warmth of his sinewy body next to hers and felt comfortable in his arms. After a dance or two, Laura was completely relaxed and let him draw her even closer, resting her head on his broad shoulder. Not since her high school days had she danced so dreamily.

"You're a good dancer, Laura," he whispered in her ear, his lips carelessly brushing against her lobes.

"I have an excellent partner who makes me forget just how rusty I am. It's been ages since I've danced a fox-trot." She was glad her voice didn't betray the slight tremors she felt at his proximity. It had also been a long time since she had been in a man's arms. Bert's purloined kiss didn't count. He hadn't really held her with any affection. It was rough possession.

"I would have thought a young lady as attractive as you would be out dancing almost every night," he commented.

"You forget . . . I'm like you . . . and have to work for a living, and also like you, I enjoy my work."

"You don't work nights too, do you?"

"About as often as you do," she countered.

"Touché," he said, smiling. "Seriously though, your job doesn't require the customer contact mine does."

"Well, for a while I attended night school and now I sometimes stay late at the museum to make sure any special exhibit I might be working on is going according to plan."

"Pity! You were born to dance." He pulled her even closer and lowered his head so his cheek could lie against hers.

When the fox-trot ended, the orchestra switched to some ragtime tunes of the early twenties.

"I'm sorry, Laura. I'm afraid we'll have to sit this one out. The music is a little before my time."

"Mine too. I wouldn't begin to know the steps involved, much less how to do them."

They sipped their wine and watched those more adept in the bunny hug and the Charleston. The knowledgeable dancers on the floor delighted and amused those who looked on in admiration, receiving a resounding round of applause after each dance. Sensing their energies were spent, the orchestra began the rousing strains of a Strauss waltz.

Laura was about to ask Kevin if he knew how to waltz when she noticed a tall, powerful figure striding across the ballroom floor, his head towering above those taking their places for the dance. He appeared to be headed their way and Laura thought he looked familiar. It took her a second or two to recognize him in his expensively tailored dark blue suit and white silk ruffled shirt. He had the air and demeanor of a Mississippi riverboat gambler, and no one could miss the steely blue eyes of Bert, the caretaker. She swallowed hard, impressed by his attire, which hinted at the strength of the form beneath it. His rough good looks were transformed into a devilish handsomeness by his apparel.

"Good evening, Mr. Courtney."

"Good evening, Bert. I must say I'm surprised to see you here. You don't usually attend our little social functions. Tired of the solitary life?" Kevin asked.

"I thought I'd see how the other half lives," Bert replied dryly, turning his eyes appraisingly at Laura. "Good evening, Miss Bickford. I trust you are enjoying yourself."

"Very much so," Laura replied in a low voice, trying not to sound giddy as spots of red rushed to settle high on her fine cheekbones. His eyes seemed to penetrate right through her, taunting her with his insolent stare. Why did he make her feel like this? So unsure of herself and confused.

"May I have the honor of this dance, Miss Bickford?"

"Well . . ." Laura looked searchingly at Kevin.

"Go ahead, Laura. I've never mastered the art of the waltz either."

As she rose from her seat, held back for her by Bert, she cringed inside. His deep, resonant voice had a strange heady effect on her. She hoped and prayed her knees wouldn't buckle when he touched her. She felt horribly conspicuous as envious female eyes followed them to the dance floor.

He put his large hand firmly on her small waist and grasped her other hand in his, and they whirled off into the midst of the other dancers. Though she tried to avoid looking at him directly, his magnetic gaze finally forced her to lift her lashes and let her eyes meet his. He smiled at her and she went all hollow inside.

"Not many young women are as competent in the waltz as you, Miss Bickford."

"It is my favorite dance, although I seldom have the opportunity to practice it." Her voice had a noticeable tremor in it and she couldn't keep the apprehension from glistening in her eyes.

"Do I frighten you?" An amused smile curled on his lips.

"Of course not. Why should you?"

"You seem a bit tense. Perhaps my dancing is not up to your expectations."

"On the contrary, you surpass them. Somehow I didn't think you capable of dancing the waltz with the expertise of a master."

"I'm capable of a number of things you aren't aware of."

Her pulse raced out of control as he continued to smile down at her, pressing his hand on the small of her back with a dominating force and spinning her round and round to the rhythms of the waltz.

Laura was dizzy and breathless when the dance ended. She felt Bert's muscular arm circle her waist tightly, steadying her. She made a motion to start back toward her table and a waiting Kevin when Bert's hand shot out, closing around her wrist like a steel vise. Before she could offer any resistance or protest, he swept her away to the strains of another waltz.

Overwhelmed by a peculiar sense of exhilaration, she relaxed and let him glide her with ease around the floor. Unconsciously she smiled at him warmly, forgetting the incident earlier in the day as the enchanted moment engulfed her.

His fingers tightened their grip on hers as his eyes lowered to gaze at her, his head remaining righteously erect.

When the dance ended, his grip on her remained steadfast. Unwillingly, she looked up at him and their eyes locked in a search for the thoughts hidden beneath them. For a fleeting second, Laura forgot there were other people present. There were only the two of them standing alone in the ballroom. The spell was broken when the orchestra started to play another fox-trot.

"Thank you," murmured Laura as he relinquished his hold on her. She was breathing rapidly. She presumed it was from the rigors of the waltz.

He took her back to the table and, with a small bow, bid them a good night. Kevin and Laura stayed for some time thereafter but, for Laura, the evening had lost its zest when she saw Bert go out the door. She danced with Kevin for several more dances but it wasn't the same. Her gaiety was a forced one.

Kevin turned the ignition off when they had reached the motel's courtyard. Laura was too deep in her own thoughts to notice the car had stopped.

"I hope you enjoyed yourself this evening," said Kevin as he slipped his arm around the back of her seat.

"It was an evening I shall never forget." Laura had a twinge of guilt. Kevin had really shown her a wonderful time but it was the waltzes with Bert that would linger in her mind forever. Kevin moved closer, making her uncomfortable. Unconsciously, she cleared her throat.

"You seem to know that man Bert quite well. What sort of person is he really?"

"Who knows what anyone is like?" Kevin mused as he slid back over into his seat.

"Miss Lawson said he worked for you at one time."

"So you've met old Hannah. I'm not surprised. She has a way of ferreting out anyone new in the area. Yes. He worked for me a couple of summers ago. A drifter of sorts, I suspect. But a darn good worker. Always on time, never drunk. No . . . I had no complaints about him. He was a loner though. Could never interest him in spending a night on the town with the boys. A dyed-in-the-wool loner. I almost dropped when I saw him at the dance this evening. And such sartorial elegance! I could hardly believe my eyes," Kevin chuckled. "And for him to dance with you was really the icing on the cake."

"What do you mean by that?"

"Well, even though nobody knew much about him, it was no secret he was not one for socializing, especially with the ladies."

"But why? A mother complex or something?"

"Nothing so Freudian. No. From what I heard it was a simple case of being jilted. Left standing at the altar despairing of an unrequited love, or so the rumor goes. I don't know if there's any truth to it. Maybe he just hasn't found the right girl yet."

"Did this happen recently?"

"I don't think so. Rumor has it it was some twelve or fifteen years ago when he was in his early twenties. Unfortunately, his distrust of women seems to have deepened during the intervening years, or so it seemed until tonight. He appeared to be quite taken with you, and who could blame him." Once again he moved closer, letting his arm encircle her bare shoulder.

"Does he have a last name?" asked Laura, her skin quivering, thinking about those moments in Bert's arms. Her emotions were taut and all muddled up.

"Last name? As I recall it was an odd one. Let me see . . . Trembling . . . no . . . Trebling. Yes, that was it . . . Trebling. Bert Trebling," he whispered as he nuzzled kisses on her neck.

Laura turned her head to say good night when his mouth came down on hers, warm and eager. His kisses were tender and prolonged. Laura wanted to respond but couldn't. There was something about Kevin that reminded her of Peter.

"I must go now. I have an early day tomorrow," she said, pulling away sharply as Bert's image flashed before her.

"But tomorrow's Sunday, a day of rest," he said, his voice thick with aroused passion and desire.

"For you perhaps, but not for me. I have to put in as much time as possible if I'm to meet my deadline."

"Can't I change your mind?" Once again he kissed her neck amorously.

Laura swallowed hard in an effort to ignore Kevin's advances. "Will you be taking me to the island tomorrow?"

"No. Sam will take you over," answered Kevin, moving away from her when he saw the moment was lost. "Maybe you work on Sunday but I don't. But I'll see you on Monday."

The next morning, Laura was not up to her usual king-size breakfast of eggs or pancakes. All she could manage was toast and black coffee.

As the boat approached the island, she stared at it with apprehension. Would he be there? Suddenly she wondered if she could face him. She decided to forget past quarrels with him and be as pleasant as she could toward him. The memory of waltzing in his arms flooded her and she didn't think it would be too difficult to be nice. Her intentions were swiftly annihilated when she entered the library.

Bert's rugged frame was emphasized by the sunlight streaming through the window and she shivered at the sight of him. His back was toward her as he stared out the window. His hands were behind his back as one hand pounded into another.

She drew in a deep breath then pleasantly said, "Good morning, Bert." It was the first time she had used his Christian name. It made her feel pushy and she was sorry the minute she let the words out of her mouth.

"Is it now?" There was a harshness in his voice she didn't understand.

"I don't follow you."

"Don't you?" He turned, his eyes ablaze with a drenching fury. "I'll admit those large amber eyes of yours brimming over with innocence had me fooled but I never thought you'd turn out to be a thief."

"A thief?" she cried, not believing what she was hearing. He must be playing some weird kind of joke on her. "What are you talking about? I've never stolen anything in my life."

"Oh, no? You've never plucked something that didn't belong to you and just spirited it away?"

Laura's anger at his outrageous accusation reached the surface and broke through. "You're insane! How dare you call me a thief!"

"Am I now? Can you deny you took something from this room?" His voice was harsh but there was an unfathomable sparkle in his blue eyes that Laura couldn't read, so she responded in kind.

"You have a lot of nerve to even suggest such a thing. I can't believe anyone could be so despicable!"

"My job is to safeguard the mansion even though it might put me in an unfavorable light. You can be assured I will have to report this to the proper authorities."

"I haven't the vaguest notion of what you're talking about. Can't you understand that?" She wasn't sure if he was serious or teasing her.

"You know perfectly well I'm talking about the missing volume on the works of Frederic Remington."

She slumped into a chair, defeat written on her face as she shook her head despondently then humbly voiced, "I only borrowed the book for something to read in the motel room."

"Borrowed? You just borrowed a priceless edition of the works of Remington? Come now, Miss Bickford, surely you can do better than that!" His cold blue eyes cut through her like sudden blasts of chilled air.

She looked up at the massive figure looming over her, her wide amber eyes giving her the look of a wounded fawn. He was a Jekyll and Hyde. This ill-dressed, ill-mannered lout bore no resemblance whatsoever to the man who had held her in his arms as they waltzed.

"I am not a thief, Mr. Trebling. The book shall be back on the shelf tomorrow," Laura said dryly, any fantasies she may have had about the man evaporated immediately. She wanted to get up from the chair but he blocked her way by standing closely in front of it. For a split second, she thought she saw a softening in his frigid eyes but his words belied any compassion.

"Can you give me any good reasons why I should trust you?"

"For heaven's sake! I never knew a man as petty and suspicious as you. Do you want me to swim back to the motel right now?" The fiery rage she felt inside was clearly evinced in her flashing eyes.

A sardonic smile played at the corners of his mouth. With his hard square jaw thrust out, he gazed at Laura steadily. "That sounds rather interesting."

"I do believe you would enjoy that. Especially if I were to be swept downstream on the way. If you don't mind I'd like to get up."

"Get up then. I'm not stopping you."

"You're standing too close."

"Does that bother you?"

"Mr. Trebling, everything about you bothers me."

"I'm delighted to hear that. I'd hate to think I was losing my charm."

"You have all the charm of a venomous, predatory reptile. Now will you please move. I have work to do even if you don't."

"I see you took the trouble to learn my name," he remarked carelessly, moving to the side of the chair.

"You know mine and I don't like being at a disadvantage." Laura rose and absently brushed down her yellow linen skirt. "By the way, how is your twin brother?"

"My brother?" Bert's dark eyebrows knitted together in an expression of utter perplexity. His eyes narrowed as he watched Laura's small graceful figure slide into the seat behind the mahogany desk, the latter dwarfing her.

"Surely that wasn't you at the dance last night."

Bert's strong laughter reverberated through the house. "Good Lord, don't tell me you wish there were two of me."

"God forbid! It must be the moon then that affects your personality. You seem to mellow at night."

"I do. Maybe you should stay on the island overnight and find out." His face became an inscrutable mask as his eyes searched her face hauntingly. He started to leave but turned and added, "Don't forget to have that book back on the shelf tomorrow."

"I wouldn't dare or you'll have me branded as a felon and jailed for life," she called after him angrily as he strode out of the room.

Laura put her elbows on the desk, pushing her hair aside and holding her head between her fragile hands. Not only couldn't she understand this strange man, but what was even more disturbing, she couldn't understand the emotions he aroused in her. Her pulse jumped alarmingly whenever he was present. It was more than his good looks, more than his virile physique; it was the man himself, a man of deep emotion, capable of violent hatred or passionate, undying love. Never before had she met a man like him.

She thought of Kevin's tender lips on hers and wondered what it would be like to be kissed by a man like Bert in warm desire instead of angry impulse. A shudder of wary anticipation trembled through her. She shook her head, determined to wipe out such notions. She'd been through all that once before and once was enough for her. Besides, she had work to do.

Once she started on the photographing and cataloging, the day passed quickly. Looking at her watch and satisfied with the day's work, she shut her radio off, packed her satchel and headed for the dock. She had just begun her descent on the marble steps when she heard Bert's voice call to her from the attic balcony above her.

"Miss Bickford . . . you needn't have the boat pick you up tomorrow evening. I have business in town and I'll take you back to the mainland."

Before Laura could reply, he had left the balcony and disappeared into his attic abode. She knew it would be futile to argue with him.

He was of the opinion his word was law and no one would have the audacity to oppose him.

When she reached the motel that evening, the first thing she did was slip the Remington book into her satchel.

CHAPTER 4

Kevin was seated at the booth when Laura came into the restaurant for breakfast.

"Good morning, Kevin," she said brightly, her spirits soaring. Was it because she was going to ride back with Bert tonight? No, it couldn't be that. It was because her work was going so well, she convinced herself. She would have to find some delicate way of telling Kevin she wouldn't be needing his services tonight, for she didn't want to hurt his feelings. "I didn't expect to see you here this morning."

"I wanted to explain why I sent Sam to pick you up last night instead of coming myself."

"You don't owe me any explanations, Kevin. Besides, you told me you didn't work on Sundays." Laura remembered how relieved she was to see Sam at the helm last night. After her encounter with Bert during the day, she really wasn't up to making light conversation with Kevin. Sam was silent during the trip back to the mainland and she had been thankful for that silence. Her thoughts were confused and she wanted to try and straighten them out but met with little success. Every time she thought she had the answer it slipped from her grasp.

"I know I said I didn't work on Sunday, but I had all intentions of picking you up last evening as a surprise. Then I found I had to complete the preliminary sketches for the Montreal commission."

"Really, Kevin, you're under no obligation to me."

"Laura, I . . ." He didn't finish his sentence. Instead he moodily stirred his coffee.

"How is it coming? Have you finished the basic design yet?" Laura asked, trying to ease his obvious embarrassment.

Kevin took a deep breath and a sip of coffee. "I hope the sketches will satisfy her. That's what I wanted to talk to you about this morning. I have to run up to Montreal after I drop you off at the island. I don't know how long I'll be there. Sam will have to pick you up tonight again."

"No problem. Mr. Trebling has business in town tonight. He said he'll bring me back," said Laura, relieved to have what might have been a difficult situation resolved so easily.

"Then you're not mad at me?"

"Of course not." She smiled happily.

"Well then, that takes care of that," he said, that boyish grin once again illuminating his face.

"It wouldn't have mattered anyway. I don't mind riding with Sam. And, as I said before, you are under no obligation to me personally. The only important thing is for me to get there and back."

"Please don't crush my ego. I was under the impression you preferred me to Sam."

Laura laughed. "I do, Kevin. But I don't want you to feel guilty if other demands on your time make it impossible."

"But I do feel guilty."

"Why should you?" asked Laura, dusting her eggs with some pepper.

"Because I keep telling you how much I want to be with you and then I go running off. I imagine it won't be too much longer and you'll be leaving."

"Probably in another three weeks, four at the most."

"Three weeks is better than nothing. I've never been in the mansion but I hope there is a mountain of material for you to take pictures of—enough for the entire summer."

"It may come to that if I don't get out of here and get started."

On the island's dock, Laura didn't see Bert watching her from the balcony as she waved good-bye to Kevin. She was exceptionally happy and hummed a tune to herself as she walked up to the door of the mansion.

When she entered the library, she took the large Remington book from her satchel. She had the edge of the heavy tome on the edge of the shelf when it slipped from her hand accidentally as the resonant voice of Bert boomed behind her, startling her.

"Returning to the scene of the crime?"

Laura spun to face him. She couldn't mask the astonishment on her face when she saw him. He was carelessly leaning against the library door jamb dressed in an open-necked white shirt, a dark blue blazer and immaculate white flannel pants that hugged his long legs. A sensuous smile eased his usual stern visage. The effect made Laura realize what a powerfully handsome man he was.

"I don't suppose I should have said that. I vowed I'd try to show

you a pleasant day today to make up for my unjust accusations of
yesterday."

Not knowing how to reply to his cautious attempt at an apology,
Laura stood mute.

"I know what you're thinking, is it me or my brother?" A hint of a
smile tugged at the corners of his wide lips.

Laura relaxed and threw him a brief smile, then stooped to retrieve the fallen book. He was next to her with one stride of his long
legs.

"Here . . . let me get that. It's heavy," he offered.

Their fingers touched on the book. Charges of electricity dispersed
themselves throughout Laura's body, scattering bands of constricting
impulses to her nerve endings. She looked at Bert and he held her
fast in his gaze. She let go of the book.

"Well, it doesn't seem any the worse for wear." His voice was
husky and she wondered if he experienced the same sensations she
did. "Shall we get started?"

"Started? For what? Where?" She was stunned by his question.

"A ride down the river to Ogdensburg."

"A ride? You know very well I can't leave here. I have work to
do."

"You worked on Sunday. Everyone is entitled to a day off."

"I'm sorry. But I must have this work done in a prescribed
amount of time."

"And if you don't?"

"I may lose my job."

"What kind of ogre do you work for?"

"He is not an ogre. Nathaniel Harte requested that everything be
cataloged before the first of July for the insurance company to give
proper coverage. I intend to carry out my assignment to the letter."

"Always the career first," he sneered.

"It's not a question of career. I took on this assignment promising
to have the job done within the time limits set by Mr. Harte and I
keep my promises."

"I won't take no for an answer. You're taking the day off and
that's that," he insisted, taking her firmly by the arm.

"And if I refuse to go with you?" she asked, her eyes flashing
defiantly at him while she was melting inside from the touch of his
hand on her bare arm.

Before Laura was aware of what was happening, he scooped her
up in his strong arms like a rag doll and proceeded to carry her out
of the house, down the incline to the far side of the island. He stood
her on her feet at the foot of a small, arched stone bridge.

"Can you manage from here?" he asked, still holding her shoulders as if he was fearful she'd flee from him.

"Do I have a choice?"

"Not really, Miss Bickford. I've made up my mind to be nice to you today. And nice I shall be."

"Even if it kills me?"

"If you want to put it that way," he laughed. "Yes."

She reluctantly walked over the foot bridge, Bert towering behind her, barring any escape.

"Huge, isn't it?" Bert's eyes scanned the vast boathouse momentarily before coming to rest on Laura.

"I've never seen anything like it before," she remarked.

He opened a side door and led her in. "Hop in." He waved his hand in the direction of a forty-two-foot cabin cruiser. Laura complied, awed by the sights around her.

With agility, Bert jumped across a mooring to start the machinery that would open the huge yacht house doors. Laura watched him, fascinated by his pantherlike movements, every muscle taut and moving with catlike precision. As the old, heavy doors creaked open, Bert jumped into the boat. She drew a sharp breath as he revved the powerful engines. In moments they were out on the river. Her thick lashes lowered and she stole glances at the tall, sinewy man at the helm. His thick dark hair rippled as the wind caught and teased it backwards.

"Why Ogdensburg?" she shouted over the roar of the engines.

"Remington."

"What?"

"Remington. You'll see." He smiled briefly.

Laura had the distinct feeling he was doing this against his will and wanted the day to be over as much as she did. She had felt used by a man before but never intimidated by one, and in a disarming way, Bert seemed to threaten her. There was a dreadful magnetism hovering about him and she was caught in its web whenever she was close to him. The morning cast shadows across his sharp, chiseled features. His face was stony, immobile, but the intense gleam in his flinty eyes kept it from being a lifeless mask. Never before had she been wary and attracted to a man at the same time. She forced her gaze to the shoreline and tried to concentrate on the passing trees and houses. Her pounding heart quietly slowed down as she observed miniature villages in the distance.

The sun flickered on her freshly shampooed hair as she lifted her tranquil face, which bore a minimum of makeup, to the brisk breeze caused by the swiftly moving boat. Her nostrils flared slightly as the morning air curled into her lungs and she licked the mist of spraying water from the soft curves of her lips. She didn't see Bert throwing her furtive glances.

The boat ride was a rare treat she hadn't expected and she pushed down the pangs of guilt that were sweeping over her for leaving the work she knew she should have been doing instead.

She once again turned her attention to the stern visage of the man steering the boat, whose narrowed eyes were now studying carefully the course of the shoal-ridden river. The artery in her neck began to throb and a weakness invade her limbs at the sight of him standing there so much in control of everything. Quickly she averted her eyes. The whole thing was ridiculous. After all, he was just another man, she tried to convince herself. She had been in a man's arms before and she had been kissed before. Why should she view him as any different from other men who had crossed her life? She wouldn't. And for her own sake, she couldn't. Never again did she want to know that horrible empty feeling in the pit of her stomach. Never again would she let a man reduce her to a mere quarry. She was her own woman and had proved her worth by the swift ascension in her chosen profession. Her dream of becoming head curator for the Metropolitan Museum of Art in Manhattan was not beyond her reach. No. She would not let either a man or her own emotions stand in the way of her ultimate objective. Whatever emotions this caretaker was kindling in her, she would handle them, relegating them to the minor position they deserved. She took a deep breath of the crisp air, pleased with her renewed sense of purpose. Again she let her eyes be captivated by the scenery scooting by.

The swift twin-engine boat sliced through the water with ease as Bert skillfully steered it through the dangerous shoals. Laura was enveloped in an uncommon exhilaration as the water sprayed past her. There was a strength, a solidity about this boat she hadn't felt in Kevin's smaller one. She quickly denied the thought that it might be the man at the helm.

"There's some coffee below. Why don't you go down and get us a cup?" Bert called to her. "I made it this morning before you came. All you have to do is heat it up."

She nodded and went down into the cabin. Her eyes widened at the size of it. It was larger than her motel room, replete with kitchen, dining area and sleeping quarters. She took a match from the holder and lit the small gas stove. While she waited for the coffee to heat, she traced her finger admiringly over the sheen of the fine mahogany table, over the tasteful curtains. When she heard the coffee beginning to churn furiously in the coffeepot, she poked her head out of the cabin and looked up at Bert. "Cream? Sugar?"

"Neither. Plain black." He gazed down at her for a moment, making her feel very small and fragile under his swift, piercing glance. She ducked her head back into the cabin, reemerging with two steaming mugs of the black brew.

Laura lowered her eyes to stare vacantly into her cup when his hand closed over hers as he took the cup from her. She didn't want him to see the confusion in them.

"Is this your boat?"

"I have the use of it," he replied curtly, then sipped his coffee.

"You make very good coffee, Mr. Trebling," she said, trying to match his efforts at friendliness.

He acknowledged her statement with a curt nod of his head. She could see her attempts at conversation were futile. She hoisted herself into the high seat opposite him and turned her attentions back to the passing scenery.

Bert maneuvered the large craft into a slip at the Ogdensburg marina with all the ease of a gull swooping through the sky.

"It's not too far from here. Several blocks or so," he said, extending his hand to her as she climbed out of the boat. The minute they were on the dock, he dropped it like a burning ember.

They walked along in silence, up one block, down another, until they were walking up the steps that led to the porch of an early nineteenth-century, wood-framed, sprawling white house that had been the home of Mrs. Frederic Remington after the death of her husband. The building was now a memorial to the late artist and housed much of his work.

Laura was in a state of euphoria, not only with the original works of Remington to behold, but also with the house itself, which had been preserved in the tradition of the nineteenth century and held numerous articles of that period.

She forgot all about Bert as she minutely studied every room, every painting, every sculpture, every article in the house. Time had no meaning for her. It wasn't until Bert came up behind her and she caught the heady scent of his masculine aftershave that she became aware of having a companion with her.

"I take it you like Remington," Bert said gruffly.

"He was a fine artist . . . and a great craftsman," Laura commented, still lost in the wonder of it all.

"Have you had your fill yet? It's a little after one o'clock and I find myself in need of some food."

"Oh, I am sorry. I didn't realize the time."

He took her arm and led her out of the house. Remington faded from her mind as the warmth of his hand cupping her elbow surged through her.

"Thank you," she said, tilting her head back to look up at him.

"For what?" His startling blue eyes seared into hers.

"For this morning."

His hand dropped to his side as they headed back toward the marina. Before getting to the docks, Bert stopped at a little fish and chips stand and waited for the white-frocked man to fill his order.

"This is the only place where they serve fish and chips as it should be served," he stated, handing her a newspaper cone filled to the brim with hot, crispy fish fillets and french fried potatoes.

"I've never seen it served like this."

"Then you've never had fish and chips. We'll take it down to the boat and I'll make a fresh pot of coffee."

They sat on the boat savoring their lunch. At first Laura felt very much at ease but was soon wishing the tall, dark, enigmatic man opposite her was Kevin, who was so easy to talk to, so easy to be with. There was an unnamed tension in the air whenever she was alone with this man and she wished her assignment was over. She wanted to go back to Brooklyn where life was uncomplicated. There her emotions were stabilized with the familiar routine of working at an absorbing job. She felt her emotional reserve ebbing as she tried to avoid the kind of relationship Bert projected in her mind. She forced herself to think of Peter in order to reinforce her determination to remain aloof from any entanglements. When they finished their coffee she was glad to hear the roar of the engines and watched with relief as they pulled away from the slip.

She had been planning in her mind how to speed up the work at the mansion. Suddenly her head spun around in bewilderment.

"You've gone by the boathouse and the mansion," she exclaimed fearfully.

"I know." His voice was calm and toneless.

"Where are we going?" She was alarmed by the thought her entire well-being was totally in the hands of this erratic and unfathomable man.

"You'll see."

Damn him, she thought. It was his answer to everything. With angry resignation, she sat back in the seat, determined not to say another word until he deposited her back at Alexandria Bay.

She sat in bitter silence as he pointed out various landmarks and misshaped houses perched precariously on minuscule shoals. Eventually, in accord with her unresponsiveness, his running commentary ceased.

Land slowly disappeared from view. Waves of panic invaded Laura as she swiveled her head about in search of a shoreline. Everywhere she looked there was nothing but water. The brute had taken her out to sea!

"Are we in the ocean?" she asked finally, her voice tight, nervous.

Bert shot her an incredulous look as if he was startled to learn she could speak. Then an inscrutable smile broadened on his sensitive lips. "Would that bother you?"

"Should it?" Laura decided to play his game of answering a question with a question and not let him see just how terrified she really was.

He hesitated before answering her. Laura waited for one of his caustic remarks. To her surprise his voice was gentle when he answered her as if sensing her fears.

"No, it shouldn't, Miss Bickford. I am a very able seaman and the boat is quite seaworthy. And as you have seen, we have all the necessary facilities on board. But to answer your earlier question. We are not in the ocean. This is Lake Ontario."

"A lake? The only lakes I have ever seen were ones where you could see the shoreline, or at least a part of it."

"When the wind whips out of the northwest, one would think they were at sea. The swells can become dangerously high. Do you enjoy boating, Miss Bickford?"

"This is the first time I've ever been on a boat like this. I think it could definitely grow on one. I like the sense of isolation it gives me," she answered truthfully. "Especially out here," she continued. "It's like there is no one else in the world. So peaceful."

"Would you like to take the helm?"

"I wouldn't know what to do."

"I'll show you. Out here you can't get into too much trouble. The river is different though. Too many shoals to contend with."

He slid out of his seat and, with a slight bow, offered it to her. She climbed eagerly into the seat still warm from his body. He leaned close to her and, giving detailed explanations, showed her the instruments for speeding up and slowing down. Laura felt the fine hairs on the nape of her neck rise at his proximity. There was a maleness about him that couldn't be denied.

"It's much like driving a car, only you control the speed with your hand," he instructed, not moving away even when she was beginning to maneuver the craft with some confidence.

She opened the throttle gradually, exhilarated by the boat's increasing speed and the feel of it as she caused it to slice through the water.

Bright with elation, she turned her clear face to him, her eyes radiant with animation as they met his. There was naked enjoyment on her face as she called to him, "Am I doing it right?"

"You're doing fine . . . just fine," he shouted back as she opened the throttle more, letting the boat skim the waves haphazardly. She gleefully turned the wheel like a child with a new toy, steering the boat over the wake of the waves she had just created.

"That way," he said, pointing a lean finger as his eyes squinted toward the west at a quickly lowering sun. He motioned for Laura to turn the boat around and head back toward the river.

He took the helm and slowed the boat down when the entrance to the river came into view.

Laura leaned back in the chair opposite him, flushed with sheer pleasure.

"I've never done anything like that before. It's a marvelous feeling. I must admit it wouldn't take me long to develop a taste for it. Such a feeling of power! Do you go out on the boat often?" she asked breathlessly.

"Only when my head needs clearing."

"Clearing of what?" she asked innocently.

"The world around me."

"Do you find the world that bad?" The sadness in his voice touched her and made her realize what a lonely man he really must be.

"Sometimes." His face was stern, tense as he headed the boat toward the unfamiliar shore. "Hungry?"

"Come to think of it, I'm famished." She glanced at her watch and was surprised to find it was almost six in the evening. The day had vanished so quickly.

"Good." He moored the boat at a small marina while Laura went below to freshen up.

Dismayed that he rushed her on board without her purse, she made do with a quick face wash. She was thankful to have found a comb in one of the drawers and wished she had some lipstick but then noticed in the mirror, the sun had brought a fair amount of color to her face. She combed the windblown and tangled hair until it bounced with sheen. It would have to do, she thought.

When she emerged, Bert was waiting on the dock after securing the boat. She took his proffered hand and jumped so forcefully, her body fell against his.

His hands grasped her shoulders with a strength that made her wince. She looked up to see a curious light in his eyes that seemed to speak of a painful resolve.

"Are you all right?" he asked, pushing her away.

"Yes," she nodded, weak and shaken from the sensation of her face against his heavy chest. She shook her head to regain her composure and stop the trickles of warmth in her blood. "I'm still famished."

He smiled crookedly and they climbed the ramp to the street.

The restaurant was small and oblong, the type indigenous to little waterfront towns where the buildings appear to be cement books forced together by unseen hands of iron. The place seated no more than twelve to fifteen people. A tired-looking waitress placed two glasses of water on the table, then absently threw down two menus before sauntering away.

Laura needn't have studied the menu so closely, for when the waitress returned to take their orders, Bert told her to bring two hamburger deluxes and coffee without even consulting her preferences.

For the most part, they ate in silence. Laura occasionally commented to Bert on the boat and the museum but he seemed too preoccupied to hear her. When they had finished eating, he hurried her back to the boat and quickly set out for Alexandria Bay.

He insisted on walking her to the motel. She wished he hadn't, for as the silence between them grew, so did the tension.

"Thank you, Mr. Trebling, for a most remarkable day," said Laura as they reached the door of her motel room.

"Then you've forgiven my unjust accusations?"

"Yes. But you were right. I never should have taken the book or anything else for that matter from the mansion. In a way, I'm glad I did though," she said mischievously, a tiny smile making its way to her lips. "Otherwise I would have never seen all those original Remington works. I am forever in your debt."

He placed his hands on her shoulders, this time gently. Her pulse quickened. Though waves of warning washed over her, she knew she wanted him to take her in his arms and forget all caution. Somewhere deep within her she wanted to succumb to the heady passion he evoked in her even though reason told her sanity must prevail. Intensely aware of his hard masculine strength as he pulled her against him, she felt herself go limp, all resistance dissipating.

His arms dropped to his sides and with a curt "Good night, Miss Bickford," he was gone.

What did she really know of this man, Bert Trebling? Or Kevin, for that matter? Nothing. No . . . it was a game she did not want to become entangled in again. The moments may be achingly sweet but the reality was unbearable. She would finish her work as soon as possible and return to the world she felt safe in, a world where only her work existed. Sleep, when it finally came, was fitful.

The morning dawned gray and misty like her spirits. After a hot shower, she dressed in a dark plaid suit with a white, lacy Dacron blouse. Everything was simple and staid, for that was how she felt. Her resolve to finish at the mansion was augmented by her strong desire to return to Brooklyn.

Sam met her at the marina and ferried her to the island. With brisk efficiency, Laura moved from object to object, her heart more in getting the job done than inspired by it.

There was no visible sign of Bert at the mansion over the next few days. Occasionally she heard noises emanating from the attic, so she knew he was present in the house. She could only assume he had eased his conscience by regaling her for a day. Now, his sense of courtesy assuaged, he wanted no further dealings or encounters with her. She couldn't make up her mind whether she was hurt or angry or relieved. She decided anger was most appropriate. He was being his obstinate and difficult self again by pretending she didn't exist.

She sat down heavily in the chair and looked down at the papers on her desk, knowing she should not let this provocative and puzzling man divert her attentions all the time.

Exasperated, she plunged furiously into the work at hand, hoping that by tomorrow she could move to the second floor, and closer to the time when she could return to the city and resume her normal activities.

The nights at the pizza parlor with her friends, where they would eat pizza or spaghetti, washing it down with chianti, until they burst. The excursions up to the Bronx Zoo and the Botanical Gardens, where they would devour their pot-luck picnic. The wishful window shopping along Fifth Avenue. And now, with the summer approaching, the early morning treks to Coney Island or Rockaway Beach to secure a small plot of sand on which to spread their blanket before the crowds arrived. All in all, and in spite of Peter, she felt herself to be very fortunate to have a job she adored and friends, male and female, with whom to share the good times in life. When it came right down to it, she was quite happy with her lot in life and really wouldn't change it. A grin tugged at the corners of her mouth as she thought about the story she would have to tell her girl friends about her exploits in the wilds of upper New York State, about the breezy Kevin and the enigmatic caretaker of the mansion.

The pencil slipped from her hand as disjointed concepts of Bert tumbled into her mind. What would she tell her friends about him? She wished there was time to get to know him better, for instinctively she knew there was a depth to the man that he cleverly cloaked by assuming a remote attitude. Sometimes when he looked at her or touched her she thought she could read and feel a tenderness toward her in those penetrating blue eyes.

She openly smiled and her heart fluttered gaily at the notion of Bert being interested in her. But it was only an illusion, for she would soon be leaving Evans Mansion and its caretaker. It would be foolish to let herself become emotionally dependent on a man she would never see again.

But then . . . it would do no harm if she allowed herself a fantasy or two about the tall, handsome man who stalked the halls and grounds of Evans Mansion.

CHAPTER 5

Laura spent a restless night, constantly tossing and turning. Going to bed with her mind in a turmoil was not in the least conducive to a sound sleep and she felt wretched. It was only six in the morning when she crept out of bed. The light filtering through the venetian blinds at the window was a hazy gray, leaving her uncertain of the weather outside.

Kevin was still in Montreal. Bert had become the invisible man, which might be a blessing, she thought, and an intense sensation of restlessness settled in her bones that even her work couldn't dispel. She promised herself a trip to Vermont to see her parents one weekend after she was back in the city.

After dressing and a quick brush of her thick, silky hair, she took a small calendar from her wallet before putting a touch of makeup on. According to her calculations, the first weekend she would have free was the third week in June. But she had a three-day holiday for the fourth of July and decided that was when she would go to Vermont. The decision eased her mind and the prospect of a visit home uplifted her spirits.

On her way to the restaurant, she stopped and bought a newspaper, thinking to read it over some leisurely cups of coffee. She had become a familiar sight there and they kept her cup full of hot coffee at no extra charge.

Sated with a hearty breakfast, she spread the newspaper out on the table and began to read the contents. She had almost an hour to wait before Sam would be at the marina.

"Miss me?"

Laura looked up in astonishment. Kevin's lilting voice and usual greeting was unmistakable. "Kevin! How nice to see you! How was Montreal this time?" she asked, thinking how attractive he was this morning.

"Empty without you. And, now that I see you again, my memory did not exaggerate your beauty and charm. In fact, it didn't do justice to them."

Laura blushed. "What are you doing here so early?"

"Looking for you. I thought I'd have to wait, but to my good fortune, you were here early too."

"Yes. I thought I'd catch up on what's going on in the world at large."

"Am I interrupting?"

"No . . . not at all. I'm happy to have some company," she replied, folding the paper and putting it on the seat beside her. "Tell me, how is the new boat coming along?"

"Better than I thought it would. The Carruthers woman is very easy to manipulate." He smiled, his hazel eyes gently appraising her.

"Do you find it amusing to manipulate women?" she asked with a hint of sarcasm in her tone.

"No. Expedient," he replied lazily. "You see, Laura, designing and building boats is an exacting craft. Most people have no conception of what is involved. They demand this should be one way, that, another. If I catered to their little whims and innovations every time they thought they had a stroke of genius, I'd end up building an unmanageable ark, totally unseaworthy. I bully them for their own good, you might say. That goes for men as well as women. I'm not a male chauvinist if that's what you're thinking." Kevin grinned at her but his eyes probed hers seductively. "What about tonight?"

"What about tonight?"

"Don't be coy, Laura. It's not like you. You know perfectly well what I mean. I want to wine and dine you."

"There's nobody I'd rather be wined and dined by." Laura was feeling impish in response to his overt interest in her.

He smiled broadly and reached for her hand. She didn't draw it away. "Laura, you're the loveliest woman I've ever seen."

"I don't think you were in Montreal at all. I think you took a quick trip to Ireland and kissed the Blarney stone, Kevin Courtney."

"With a colleen as fair as you I don't need the magic of the Blarney stone to sing your praises," he retorted, squeezing her hand affectionately.

"Your flattery is beguiling but really, it is beginning to embarrass me."

"Modest to the core. Will your virtues never end?" He threw his hands in the air in a gesture of feigned wonder, making Laura laugh aloud. His good looks were augmented by his charm and easy amiability.

"Why don't we both play hooky today. After all, I haven't seen you for some time. And knowing your penchant for work, you probably haven't had your nose out of that dusty old mansion since I've left. What do you say?"

"It sounds tempting—"

"But?" he interrupted.

"Yes . . . there is a but. I'm going to start on the second floor today and I don't want to postpone it another day. I've looked forward to the move for some weeks now and don't want to let it go for another minute. I'll take a rain check on your kind offer though."

"I'll hold you to that, Miss Bickford. Are you ready to go? You even have me anxious to see you finish up on that island. Then maybe you'll find a whole day on your hands with nothing to do and I can claim it."

Laura leaped onto the dock when they reached the island. Kevin took her hand and gallantly kissed it. He turned it over and placed a lingering kiss on her palm. "Till tonight," he called as the boat veered back to the mainland.

For several minutes, she stood on the dock watching the small motorboat be reduced to a speck in the distance before she headed for the mansion.

She found Kevin Courtney pleasant, amusing and easy to be with. Everything about him combined appealingly and seemed to be natural attributes rather than affectations he purposely cultivated. She genuinely liked him but that was as far as it went. His touch was pleasant but it didn't send her pulse racing wildly. He didn't have and never would have that magnetic power over her that the caretaker evoked. No . . . nobody had any power over her, she warned herself, yet she was powerless to stop her eyes from glancing upward toward the attic, hoping for a glimpse of the man she had to train herself to ignore and forget.

Whether her imagination was playfully teasing her, she didn't know, but there appeared to be—for a fleeting second—a shadowy form at the attic window staring down at her. She shook her head absently to clear it of the ghostly image it had conjured up. With firm steps, she trod up the incline and proceeded into the interior of Evans Mansion.

The achy tiredness that had gripped her earlier was dissolving. Her spirits and body were reenergized as she tackled the time-consuming task of moving everything upstairs. With an air of elated satisfaction, she looked around, pleased with herself at having accomplished it all before noontime. She had even begun to lay out a plan of procedure for the second floor cataloging.

"Are you there, girl?" Hannah Lawson had marched into the library. Her eyebrows arched to find it empty. "Where the devil are you, Laura?" she shouted.

"Up here, Miss Lawson," called Laura, making her way to the wide marble staircase.

"Ah, I was beginning to think I was going dotty in my old age. I swore I saw young Courtney bring you over to the island."

"I've moved everything to the second floor."

"The work's progressing then?"

"Yes. It won't be long now."

"You sound anxious to leave us."

"I'll have to admit I'm a bit homesick."

"Gracious! How remiss I've been. You must lunch with me today. I won't take no for an answer. I feel as though I've been neglecting you."

"Miss Lawson—"

"Hannah!" the patrician woman demanded.

"Hannah," Laura said softly. "You shouldn't feel that way."

"I said I'd have you to lunch and I will. A Lawson always keeps her word. I've been in New York besieged with lawyers and stockbrokers. Leeches! All of them!" Hannah threw her hands in the air imperiously. "They should be outlawed! A blot on society! I don't want to think about them. Especially before I eat. They cast nothing but clouds on a sunny day."

"I hope you didn't find bad news in New York."

"No. On the contrary, some old stocks I had have taken on some new importance. They are going to pay some dividends for a change. But right now, lunch is the most important thing I can think of. Get your things, girl, and let's go."

Laura ran back upstairs to retrieve her purse, then followed Hannah to the dock.

Hannah's house was, indeed, most peculiar. Laura had never really noticed it on her many trips back and forth to the island. Perhaps it was because it was partially hidden by heavy pine trees. It resembled a castle keep complete with a facade of dull gray stones. A solitary tower nestled in a grove of thick evergreens.

The first floor consisted of nothing more than a kitchen and a living room. The second, a bedroom and the third, a study or library, Laura couldn't tell which.

"Well . . . what do you think of my little refuge?" asked Hannah after giving Laura the grand tour, with undeniable pride in her manner.

"Charming . . . truly charming and very clever architecture," replied Laura, moved by genuine admiration. "You have some fabulous antiques here."

"Never really thought of them as antiques. To me, they're only the family hand-me-downs."

"There are several pieces whose worth might run into the thousands," Laura commented.

Hannah shrugged as she led the way back downstairs by means of a circular staircase and out into the kitchen, then onto an outdoor terrace. Laura found herself seated in a wrought-iron chair on the patio where light and shadow played whimsically on the multicolored flagstones. A path wound its way through the pines down to the dock. From the patio, she could see the sun turn the lapping water to sparkling jewels.

The table before her was elegantly set. Doulton china trimmed with blues and golds, lead crystal glasses and solid sterling silverware. She hefted the knife thinking of her own inexpensive stainless steel flatware at the apartment. Her whole set didn't weigh as much as that knife, she mused.

"I hope you brought your appetite with you, young lady," Hannah said as she placed a bowl of fresh salad on the table, then poured a dry white wine into the delicately etched crystal glasses.

"You set an exquisite table, Hannah."

"I don't care much for eating. I like to dine. With all of man's innovations and intellectual achievements, I find paper plates and plastic utensils the most debasing. Absolutely inhuman and uncivilized to say the least."

Laura tried to conceal a smile as she sipped the light wine and sampled her crisp salad.

"Tell me about yourself, Laura. Are you a native New Yorker?"

Between bites and sips, Laura told Hannah of her childhood in Vermont and her good fortune in finding a job to her liking so quickly when she moved to the city. Hannah listened intently, interrupting occasionally with pointed questions.

"And now an assignment that is truly your own. Quite an accomplishment for one so young." Hannah filled Laura's glass with more wine and, picking up the empty salad plates, headed back into the kitchen.

"Can I help you with anything, Hannah?"

"No . . . no, child. Stay right where you are. I won't be but a minute."

She returned to the patio carrying a large silver salver where two succulent roasted Cornish game hens slept on a bed of rice pilaf which, in turn, was surrounded by a variety of hot vegetables.

"Oh, Hannah, that looks too good to eat," exclaimed Laura, her mouth starting to water at the savory aroma.

Laura surprised herself by the amount of food she consumed. The wine seemed to clear her palate, preparing the way for additional morsels.

"Hannah, that was superb! Henri, the chef, has a serious rival in you."

"Oh, you've been to Rostand's?"

"Yes. Mr. Courtney was good enough to take me."

"Fine lad. A bit overambitious though."

"It seems to me he is a very hard worker," Laura defended him.

"Oh . . . touched a nerve, have I? Are you smitten by the young man?" Hannah displayed an amused smile.

"I find him very personable and a thoughtful companion. Nothing more." Laura would have been annoyed if someone else had asked her that. But somehow coming from Hannah, she didn't mind. Hannah was an open, forthright woman who was used to saying exactly what was on her mind. By the same token, her replies were always honest and to the point.

"And handsome. You didn't add handsome."

"Yes, he's quite good looking," Laura laughed, then after a pause said more seriously, "Why have you never married, Hannah?"

"Came close once. Too close. He was a striking man, the proverbial tall, dark and handsome. The caretaker over at the mansion reminds me of him in many ways. Yes . . . I was quite taken with him. A dreamy-eyed simp of a young girl dazzled by the sophisticated charms of an older man. When he asked for my hand in marriage, the world exploded into a million bubbles of sunshine for me. My parents, of course, had their misgivings. It took several months of cajoling on my part before they consented to our marriage.

"The date was set, the invitations sent out. Oh, it was to be the social event of the year. A few weeks before the wedding my father called me into his study. I shall never forget the look of anguish on his face." Hannah paused, her eyes glazed with poignant memories. It was several moments before she spoke again. "Anyway, to make a long story short, my father informed me my intended had left a wife in Europe somewhere a number of years ago, never bothering to get a divorce.

"I tried to override his accusations with rash protestations of undying love—all the wild twitter that a naïve young girl could think of. But my father was adamant. When my ranting became intolerable to him, he vociferously expanded the picture of my fiancé. All the time he had been paying court to me, he was frequently seen in the company of other women. I can still hear my father shouting 'Womanizer!' It sounded very evil at the time and I was crushed. A woman staying somewhere in Europe had no meaning for me. She was unseen, unknown, unfelt by me. But on my own ground, with women whose names I recognized and while he was wooing me, was more than I could bear. I was beaten and my father knew it. The wedding was duly canceled."

Laura's heart went out to the older woman. She felt she knew how it must have been for her. She recalled the devastation she felt learning the true nature of Peter.

"There must have been others later on," she said warmly.

"There were many others. But I could never bring myself to trust them. Oh, I did have some pleasant romantic interludes but if they looked like they might become serious, I'd flee like a frightened rabbit. But enough of yesteryear. When will you be going back to the city?"

"In a few more weeks I should have the second floor completed. Then I'll head home if all goes well."

"Do you expect it won't?"

"No," laughed Laura. "Unless something dire happens. I'd hate to have my camera smashed or my hands broken at this stage of the game."

"My, those are rather dire extremes. Tell me, does the caretaker disrupt your concentration?"

"No," she fibbed. "I hardly see him. He stays in his rooms in the attic for the most part. Once in a while I see him around the grounds tending to this or that. We pretty well steer clear of each other."

"I don't blame him."

"Why?" asked Laura, distress registering on her face.

"Alone in that old mansion with a pretty young thing like you. The man must have a will of iron."

"I'm afraid we don't get along too well. He has a very irascible disposition. Besides, I've been told he has a strong antipathy to women in general."

"I know. Pity though. He's such an attractive devil."

"I hate to eat and run, Hannah, but I really must get back."

"Of course, my dear. I'll take you back over but finish your wine first."

"Can't I help you clean up before I go?" asked Laura, draining the dregs from her glass.

"No. I don't trust anyone with my Doulton. Besides, you are a guest and I don't make my guests work for their supper."

"The lunch surpassed all my expectations. You're a very exceptional cook, Hannah."

"Thank you, my dear. You must come and lunch with me again before you leave."

"I'd be delighted."

Laura swung her satchel by her side, feeling not only lighthearted but a bit light-headed from the wine as she climbed the incline to the mansion.

Inside, she clicked on her little transistor radio and began her work on the second floor. She switched on the strong floodlight to illuminate the object she intended to photograph. It didn't light up! In frustration she started to haul it downstairs to the library to see if the bulb was defective when she remembered Hannah telling her about the electricity at the mansion. There was no power on the second floor! The thought of hauling each item up and down the stairs seemed like an appalling waste of time. If only she had some extension cords, the solution would be perfectly simple. She could pick some up in town. But dismayed at the thought of losing an entire afternoon, she decided to beard the lion in his den. There had to be some in the mansion somewhere, what with all the work that had been done on the mansion recently. It was worth a try.

Her heart pounded as she mounted the stairs to the attic floor, whether from fear or excitement, she couldn't tell. She forced herself to rap lightly on the closed door. There was no answer so she rapped harder.

The door swung open. It was obvious from the expression on Bert's face she was not wanted there.

"What brings you here?" he asked irritably.

"I need some electricity on the second floor."

"There is none," he growled and started to close the door.

"I know that," fumed Laura, exasperated by his mercurial insolence. "I was wondering if there were any extension cords around."

With a resentful sigh, Bert slipped out and shut the door behind him with a slam of annoyance. "I thought you career women were totally self-sufficient."

"I wouldn't have bothered you if it weren't necessary. I don't want to waste the entire afternoon and I need the lights to continue my work." Her voice was sharp.

"I'll be glad when you finish up around here and stop disturbing me." He started down the stairs.

"Believe me, nobody will be happier than I to get the job done with and return home. And it'll be the happiest day of my life when I don't have to deal with the likes of you," she cried, darting after him.

"Anything to get you out of here. If extension cords will expedite your departure then I'll move heaven and earth to find some for you," he hissed through clenched teeth.

He opened a door off the main dining room revealing a butler's pantry, then opened a cabinet door and removed a flashlight. Laura noticed there were a number of different types of flashlights in the cabinet.

"Where are you going?" she asked.

"To get your damn extension cords, Miss Bickford. They're in the basement. I suppose you're going to follow me even though it is not necessary," he snapped and glowered at her.

"I would like to see the kitchen and the substructures," she replied, trying to keep the pleading tone out of her voice.

"Come along then. But mind you, stay close to me. Some of the sections down there are quite dark and dangerous."

She followed him down the cold gray stone steps, which immediately opened up on a vast room dominated by a long, wide wooden table. Muted light filtered in from the half windows perched high on the walls above ground level.

"Here's your kitchen. The extension cords are at the other end of the basement. The workmen kept most of the tools in the back storeroom. Here, take my hand. It can get very dark along these inside corridors."

As his large, warm hand closed over hers, she tensed. The flesh of his hand pressing against hers staggered her and the touch sent agitated flutters of untapped responses deep within her, responses that even Peter's fervent kisses never aroused. Her hand clung to his, not in fear of the unknown darkness, but with an intangible longing.

"Here we are," he said as he flashed the light from one corner to the next. "Ah . . . your extension cords."

He lifted several large coils of wire from a wooden peg on the wall and slung them over his broad shoulder, motioning for her to follow him.

Laura desperately tried to keep up with his lengthening stride. But he turned a corner too sharply and suddenly everything was black. She stumbled along, trying to feel her way along the growing maze of clammy walls. Groping blindly, she tried to regain her sense of direction when she heard Bert's voice cut through the inkiness. "Stop where you are."

She felt a steely arm encircle her waist and a flash of light revealed a cavernous, gaping square hole just in front of her. One more step and she would have been at the bottom of it. She turned and threw her arms around her protector in horror.

"Oh, my God! What in heaven's name is that?" she cried, terrified.
"An empty swimming pool. This place didn't lack for grandeur. Are you all right?" he asked with genuine concern.

Lost in a wave of uncertainty and verging on panic, she pressed herself against his formidable chest and whispered, "Take me out of here."

Bert's muscular arms clamped her to his lean, hard body, which she felt tense at the intimate contact. Her brain told her to disengage herself immediately but her body seemed to have a will of its own and refused to budge from his powerful form as she shivered against him.

"You're trembling," he whispered huskily.

"I've never been so frightened. I thought I had lost you."

He pulled her closer, caressing her soft hair with his cheek. The flashlight pointed downward, casting a peculiar light in the subterranean room. "I'm here now," he murmured.

Impulsively Laura increased her hold on him, sending odd waves of desire through her, craving him without reserve while every nerve in her body wanted him to kiss her, to feel those warm exciting lips once again mingling with hers.

She heard the brief thud as the extension cords fell to the cement floor. Shadowy images disappeared as he shoved the flashlight into his back pocket. It didn't matter that all around them was nothing but an inky void. She had already lost track of the real world. Nothing existed except the scent of the man who was enfolding her in his arms, pressing her to his taut body.

A twinge ran over the top of the delicate hairs on her arms causing them to bristle to attention as his softly pursed lips caressed each of her eyelids and slowly traced a path over her cheeks, then languidly savored the soft flesh of her neck. A small moan escaped her lips as her hands found their way into the black mass of hair on his head.

Like a starving man's, his mouth came down hard on hers, hungrily devouring the taste of her parted lips, then moving over them with unexpected tenderness, igniting a tempestuous flame within her. It was the kind of moment she had always dreamed about. He was now the gentle, passionate man she knew he tried so hard to disguise.

His hand came to lovingly cradle her head as if he feared he might lose it in the dark while his other hand feathered up and down the curve of her spine sending rhythmic spasms to her nerve endings, making them leap with pleasure and desire. She leaned into him, her being filled with a rapture that sent her head spinning in all different directions. She didn't know what was happening to her and she really didn't care. Time, reality, the very earth itself ceased to exist for her.

When his mouth left hers vanquished, she kept her face turned upward in anticipation and longing for an even more deadly assault on her lips. It never came. Her eyes fluttered open to the blackness around them in dumb wonder as his hands rubbed lightly over her shoulders with hesitation, as if he was uncertain of his own mind. His fingers skimmed softly over her cheek before his lips pressed fondly on her forehead; then he released her. For a moment she thought he was going to speak as she felt the warmth of his breath fan her ear. She swallowed hard in expectation of some endearing words from his lips, but none came.

With the flashlight once again in hand, he bent down, scooped the coiled extension cords back on his broad shoulder and swung the illuminating beam down the corridor that would lead them out of the labyrinth. As if nothing had happened he took her hand in his and walked through the dim corridors as Laura trudged behind him.

She felt as though she had willingly let someone punch her in the stomach and was now regretting her eager foolishness. Her fingers went to her burning lips as she repented her uncustomary and rash behavior. It wasn't like her to yield with such utter abandon, displaying an aggressiveness she didn't know she possessed. Her fingers left her lips to feel the hot flush on her cheeks. What was the matter with her anyway? She felt like a naughty schoolgirl who had let some simp of a youth have his way with her on their first date. It was ridiculous! She had only been kissed yet she felt as though her very soul had been raped. She had to get over this feeling of wantonness before the bright light of day was upon them. The thought of the caretaker seeing the confused turbulence on her reddened face and the uncertainty in her eyes would shame her. She was a grown woman and had to handle the situation for what it was—a kiss she had given out of fright to a man who had rescued her. It was as simple as that. But was it?

It wasn't a kiss of gratitude she had given him when his lips met hers. Nor was it given out of fright. She had responded to the man and the desire he had created within her. Even now she could hear her heart pounding in her ears as his strong hand held hers so firmly, making her light-headed with a rare kind of joy. No. It wasn't simple. It was the most complicated feeling on the face of the earth. But it was delicious.

She watched the flashlight's beam bounce along the dark corridor forming shadows much like the doubts that were creeping into her mind. Raising her glance to the towering figure leading her out of the inky maze, she felt safe and secure in the knowledge that no matter how caustic he might become verbally, he would never let her come to any harm. He held her hand with a protective warmth that belied his sometimes indifferent manner.

As the hazy light of the vast kitchen came closer, she drew a deep breath. Entering the kitchen, Bert threw her a glance over his shoulder. She forced an impassive expression onto her face to match his expressionless countenance.

Back on the first floor, she felt empty and drained watching the dark leonine head and healthy masculine figure uncoil and run the extension cords from the live sockets downstairs to the electrical void of the second floor. Neither of them had spoken a word since their lips had met in the dark and parted so unexpectedly. Laura was thankful for the respite, which gave her time to collect her thoughts and emotions. In the cold light of day, what happened down in the basement seemed remote and took on a dreamlike quality.

"You have power now," he informed her tonelessly when he had finished, not even turning to face her as he spoke.

"Thank you," she whispered. His deep resonant voice had cut through her, shaking her nerves awake to the fact the kiss had been real—all too real.

He nodded and left without so much as a glance in her direction.

She didn't know how she managed to get any work done during the rest of the afternoon. Her hand would tremble or her mind would wander. But she did take a few photographs and scribble some notes. Most of the time she spent glancing at her watch, wanting the hands to move to six o'clock, when she would be taken off the island and away from the disturbing presence of the caretaker. Just knowing he was hovering about the premises made her ill at ease and unsure of herself, a condition she never had to deal with before.

At ten minutes to six, she sighed audibly, picked up her satchel with her purse and headed for the dock. Halfway down the marble steps, she turned, compelled to look up at the attic balcony.

Arms spread and hands braced on the railing, the hunched figure of Bert stood watching her. Their eyes locked with mutual yearning and Laura had to quell the impulse to run back into the mansion, back into Bert Trebling's arms.

She broke the visual contact and ran to the dock as fast as she could.

CHAPTER 6

Laura took a steaming hot shower in the hopes it would wash away the memory of Bert's body crushing against hers. Never would she let herself be mesmerized by that man again. She was glad she would be spending the evening with Kevin. The prospect of being alone in the motel room was dreary; it gave her too much time to think. Kevin was a man she could understand and deal with on her own terms.

She applied her makeup and perfume with care and delicacy. Looking in the mirror, she was satisfied with her appearance. The pale blue linen dress she had purchased as a treat in one of the small dress shops in Alexandria Bay complemented her coloring. She twisted back and forth to observe the effect of the flared skirt.

"Do you have any idea how delectable you are?" asked Kevin with unabashed admiration shining in his eyes as he opened the car door for her.

"You're impossible, Kevin," she chided with a lilt in her voice. She felt so at ease with him and was looking forward to the evening, hoping it would erase the emotions Bert had stirred within her.

Henri himself greeted them warmly. And the meal that followed was a revelation of the culinary arts. Mussels and squid in a tangy, hot sauce, a leek and lentil soup delicately graced with herbs, a veal cordon bleu that excited even the dullest of taste buds.

"I think Henri has taken a fancy to you, Laura," teased Kevin. "He only serves mussels and squid to a select clientele. Well, I'm afraid he'll have to get in line behind me. Any firm romantic commitments in the city?"

"No," answered Laura, shaking her head. "And I don't intend to make any."

"That sounds ominous."

"It wasn't meant to be. It's just that . . . well, if you stick your hand in a fire and it gets burned, you don't go and stick it in again."

"A fire can be warming. One doesn't have to get burned, you know," he countered with a smile that Laura found engaging.

She didn't like the turn of their conversation. Kevin had a penchant for getting personal, she thought, and quickly changed the subject before it became too personal.

"I had lunch with Hannah Lawson the other day. She's quite a chef and could easily be a strong rival for Henri."

"I don't think Henri has to worry about Hannah opening a restaurant. She's too busy counting her money most of the time."

"Oh, Kevin, don't be ridiculous. I know she has some stocks, but with inflation and all it's hard for older people to keep up with the spiraling cost of living."

Kevin sat back in his chair and gave himself up to unbridled laughter. Finally he gained control of himself but the gaiety remained in his eyes.

"That old Hannah is something else! She'd have everyone around here believing she's on the verge of applying for welfare. Well, my dear Laura, I know better. Hannah Lawson is an extremely wealthy woman. She has shares in AT&T and Dupont that were purchased at the selling price of thirteen to twenty cents a share back in the days of the great depression. Her real estate holdings would make an Arabian emir look like the owner of a five-room ranch in Levittown. Your kindly old Miss Lawson is a shrewd, calculating businesswoman whose ambitions have rendered her one of the wealthiest women alive. Of course, she had a noble start from her father, a millionaire in his own right. Old Hannah parlayed that pittance into an empire."

Laura was stunned. Hannah did not impress her as a mogul of the business world. But there was no reason for Kevin to lie. There was too much sincerity in his voice for her to doubt him. She thought of those priceless antiques that Hannah had shrugged off as inconsequential. If she were truly hard up, the sale of only one of those pieces would keep her in comfort for some time. Laura found the whole thing puzzling.

"If she is as well off as you say she is, why does she live so frugally on that island?"

"On the island, she does. It's a game she plays for the summer. Where she really shows her colors is in her town house in Manhattan or in her villa in Bermuda. Don't get me wrong. She's not a bad person if you can stand her blunt and imperious manner."

"I think that's part of her charm. Besides, her bearing is so regal one would be disappointed if she didn't display those traits."

"I wouldn't be surprised if those very traits have kept her a spinster all these years. With her money, she could have caught herself a handsome, dashing man. But I suspect she is the type who wants to keep all that dough to herself. Now you, Laura, are different. I can tell you're the giving type. Warm and generous." His voice softened as he leaned forward in the chair and placed his hand over hers.

His words brought Hannah's poignant story of her brief love affair to Laura's mind. Of all people, she knew, it was the warm generous kind who got hurt the most when that trust was betrayed. She was glad the restaurant was dimly lit as tears were starting to well in the corners of her eyes. She felt uncomfortable, as if the dining room was closing in on her, suffocating her.

"Excuse me," she said, rising from her seat. "I'll only be a minute."

"Don't be long. I have a surprise for you and we'll have to hurry if we're to get there on time," cautioned Kevin as he glanced at his watch.

He deftly edged the car close to the pier where a large white boat gently rocked in the water, its brightly colored lights shimmering on the rippling waters. Laughter and music filled the still night air.

"What is it?" Laura asked as he opened the car door for her.

"The Mary Belle. A veritable floating night club. Three hours of mirth and merriment while cruising up and down the river. I'm only sorry she's not a paddle wheel—then we could conjure up visions of the old south. Scarlett and Rhett, you know. Come on, let's get aboard before she sails without us." He grabbed her hand and they raced up the boarding ramp.

Laura was a little out of breath by the time they reached the main salon. The small orchestra was in full swing as they pulled away from the pier with several loud blasts from the ship's bowels announcing their departure. Hors d'oeuvres, hot and cold, and drinks were plentiful. Kevin introduced her to a number of people and they all sat at a large oblong table. Everyone was most convivial as they danced, drank, ate and talked. Even though the room was becoming stuffy and hot, she couldn't remember when she had had a better time or laughed so much. Kevin looked at her thoughtfully.

"If you'll excuse us, I think we'll take a stroll on deck and clear our heads of some of this smoke. What do you say, Laura?"

"Sounds great."

The cool evening breezes played with her shoulder-length hair, wisping it around her small oval face. Kevin's fingers tenderly pushed back some of the stray tendrils. He gazed into her warm amber eyes and, taking her head between his hands, kissed her with deep tenderness. Laura responded, not with passion, but fondly. She wished she could match his ardor but it just wasn't in her.

"You're not going to be here much longer, are you?" he asked softly, running the back of his thumb along her fine jawbone.

"No. Another week or so," she replied.

"Then I'm coming to New York City," he stated flatly.

"Kevin, we hardly know each other." She stood back but his arm drew her closer to him.

"That's what I intend to correct," he murmured as he kissed the tender part of her neck.

"Let's go in and join the others."

"Afraid of me?"

"No . . . not really. You're kind and sweet. But I'm not ready for this yet."

"The fire?"

"Yes. The fire."

"I've got time. Besides, I haven't been to the big city in ages. I'm about due." He pulled her arm through his and leisurely headed for the salon. "Did you know there are a number of potential yacht commissions sitting around Manhattan just waiting for someone to scoop them up?"

"I can picture yachts sailing up and down the East River."

"Don't laugh. Most of those budding executives, and the established ones too, have expensive homes on Long Island Sound and are dying to be the first ones to have a yacht designed exclusively for them."

Before Laura could answer him, they were at the table, where a heated discussion of politics was raging and they were quickly drawn into it.

On the way back to the motel, Kevin seemed preoccupied, so she remained quiet. She had some thinking of her own to do. She knew she should curb Kevin's persistent pursuit but didn't know quite how to go about it without hurting his feelings. Yet she wondered if it would hurt his feelings. He never seemed to take things seriously anyway and he had warned her of his inconstant nature when it came to women.

"What did you think of Jenny Tyler?" Kevin asked, breaking the silence as if he had read her mind.

"Which one was she? I'll have to admit I'm a little weak connecting names with faces."

"She was the one staunchly defending the environmentalists."

"Oh, yes. A very pretty and vivacious young woman. Why do you ask?"

"She was my fling, so to speak, last summer. Quite a girl!"

Laura could see him grin in the dim light of the car. "If you think so much of her, why did you break it up?"

"She got that 'I want to get married' look in her eye. Other than that . . ." His voice trailed off and he shrugged.

"Then you really meant what you said about no commitments." Her conviction about his capriciousness was strengthened.

"Of course. I have too many places to go and too much to do to be hamstrung by a clinging female. That's why I took to you right away. You don't seem to have that attribute."

Laura stared out the car window. She couldn't think of a reply to his remark.

"What's the matter, Laura? Did I say something wrong?" Kevin asked, glancing at her briefly.

"No . . . not at all."

"Good. I didn't think you were the kind of person who would be offended by candor. By the way, Sam will be doing the honors for a few days. I have to slip back to Montreal and get to know my client's personality a little better. She's a very complex young woman and I want to make sure I understand every facet of her delicate nature."

"Sounds like you enjoy your work," said Laura with amusement, surprised by her total lack of jealousy.

"I sure do. I meet an awful lot of people in my job. Meeting you was an unexpected bonus. Well, here we are, fair lady. Your palace awaits." He kissed her good night somewhat absently as if his mind had already fled to Montreal and the prospects there. However, he did wait until she was safely inside her motel room.

For the next few days, Sam took her to the island. When she inquired about Kevin, he only muttered, "Workin'."

Once on the island she went about her business with a sense of uneasiness. She knew Bert was lurking about and it disturbed her. At the smallest sound she would turn expecting to see his powerful frame in the doorway and his hypnotic eyes staring at her. But when she did turn around, no one was there. Why did this aloof, reticent enigmatic man enchant her so when there was someone like Kevin to pay her every courtesy? She rubbed her eyes with the back of her hands as if it would give them some mystical insight. She walked to the window of the nearest parlor hoping to rejuvenate her ardor for work.

She vaguely scanned the vista before her. The window had a commanding view of the island. A half-naked figure, clad only in ragged cut-off jeans, crossed her visual path. The tall, sinewy form could only be that of the caretaker. Her curiosity grew as she watched him carry large crates into what was once the powerhouse. His muscles rippled with controlled strength as he moved the heavy burden. It must be some of that new equipment Hannah had told her about that would help generate electricity. She shivered knowing the fascination was not for the equipment but for the man. She couldn't take her eyes from him. No man had ever had such an effect on her, not even Peter. She watched his dark hair stir in the breeze and her emotions became saturated with confusion. Why did he attract her so? Was this what falling in love was like? No. She couldn't possibly be in love with a man she hardly knew. She walked away from the window determined to complete the cataloging as quickly as possible and return to Brooklyn.

The following day Hannah appeared, insisting Laura dine with her again.

Hannah Lawson rowed her small boat with the earnest vigor of a Harvard oarsman pitted against a rival from Yale. Her back was rigid, and not a gray hair was out of place. Her face, free of any makeup, had a healthy glow about it. Laura liked this brusque woman and would miss her greatly when she returned home.

"Won't be long now, will it, Laura?" Hannah asked as she laid the platters of food on the table. "Your work will be done and you'll be leaving us."

"I'm afraid you're right, Hannah."

"Do I detect a note of remorse in your voice? Young Courtney perhaps? Or is it the inscrutable caretaker of Evans Mansion?"

Laura smiled. "You're a very astute woman. And I wish I could give you an answer but I don't have any answers myself regarding the gentlemen in question. I wish I did. One thing I do know, I shall certainly miss you, Hannah. I've found the few times we've been together will make very pleasurable memories for me. In a way, I envy your self-sufficiency and assuredness."

"Neither of which I have, you know. I have moments when I'm not too sure about anything. I come up here to regroup. Then, too, some of my friends have homes here and we all delight in getting away from the humidity and razzle-dazzle of the city and getting down to some serious bridge or poker."

"Poker?" Laura had a hard time visualizing the stiff-back Hannah playing a chancy game of poker.

"You know, it's funny," Hannah began, her face screwed up in a frown. "But I've noticed the women take their bridge seriously and the men become demoniacal about poker."

"You play poker with the men?"

"Definitely. I can read their faces like an open book," Hannah declared proudly.

"Anyone in particular?" Laura asked impishly.

"Gracious no! I'm too old for that nonsense!"

"One is never too old for love, Hannah."

"I'm the one who should be waxing wise about love, not you, dear girl." Hannah's laugh was deep and throaty. "Good heavens, girl, I'm in my sixties! Maybe when I was in my fifties, I could have entertained such a thought. But now? Oh, come, Laura."

"Jennie Jerome, Winston Churchill's mother, had a twenty-four-year-old suitor when she was in her sixties," Laura argued.

Hannah now burst into gales of laughter, downed her glass of wine in one gulp and replied, "Number one, I'm not Jennie Jerome. Number two, I could never take a twenty-four-year-old seriously."

"There are some very dashing men in their sixties and seventies," Laura persisted, starting to feel the heady effects of the wine.

"I have the feeling, young lady, that you've fallen in love and can't wait until everyone else you know is in love too." Hannah's eyes sparkled with amusement as she watched Laura blush profusely. "There are all kinds of love in this world and, believe me, I've had my share."

"I . . . didn't . . . well . . . I'm not . . ." Laura began to stammer but found she couldn't put her thoughts into words that made any sense. She had to divert the conversation away from her own confused emotional state.

Hannah twirled the delicate stem of the wine glass in her hand thoughtfully. Laura continued her argument with a bravery gleaned from the wine. "You could travel and meet all kinds of people. I know money is no problem."

"What do you mean money is no problem?" Hannah's eyes narrowed suspiciously.

"Kevin told me you are a very wealthy woman. I can't understand why you isolate yourself on this island away from the world," Laura said in all innocence, taking another sip of the fruity wine and not believing she was actually talking in so brash a manner.

"Courtney," mused Hannah reflectively. "If I told you he was fabricating, who would you believe?"

"It really doesn't matter to me, Hannah. I like you just the way you are, rich or poor."

Arching her eyebrows, Hannah smiled wryly. "For some reason I believe you."

"Would you mind if I came to visit you here next summer when I get some vacation time?" asked Laura. The wine had made her forward and bold, which was totally out of character for her. Nevertheless, she sipped again at the wine.

"I'd be delighted, my dear. But we don't have to wait until then. I will be returning to the city around the first of September. I'll give you my address and telephone number there before you leave the islands. It's a small town house on East Thirty-sixth Street."

"Great! Then I can take you out to lunch. Several lunches, in fact."

"We'll see about that."

"You only come here for the summer then?"

"Yes. Peace and quiet. No servants hovering about and I can let my hair down and do as I please."

"For once, I shall be looking forward to the winter in the city."

"Don't get your hopes too high, my dear. Come December, I usually head for Bermuda, returning to the city again in March or April."

Disappointment flooded Laura and she looked down into her lap. As she did, she noticed the time on her watch and was startled to see how late it had grown. "Oh, Hannah, I must get back. I've been here longer than I should," she exclaimed, rising from the chair.

"My. You are conscientious, aren't you? Well, a good row after lunch is always beneficial to the digestion."

Languidly Laura trailed her hand in the water, soothed by the gentle lapping of the waves. Hannah's strokes were strong and vigorous as she plowed the small boat through the slightly choppy waters. It was almost incongruous to watch the patrician grand dame pulling the oars of the frail wooden craft. But it gave Laura a sense of peace, a sense of well-being. Or was it the wine? She had drank more than she was accustomed to and it had been a heavy, fruity wine, the kind that gets into the bloodstream rapidly.

"I can see why you come here, Hannah. Everything is so simple here. Food and shelter seem to be the only real, important necessities in life."

"In a way they are. But you're forgetting a very necessary ingredient to human survival."

"Oh?" Laura questioned dreamily.

"Companionship. Humanity needs humanity. You've got to admit dining with friends or loved ones is far preferable to dining alone. Don't you agree?" asked Hannah, pulling on the oars in steady cadence.

Laura nodded, then murmured, "I suppose so."

"Oh, how I wish you were staying in the Islands for the entire summer. There are so many things you haven't seen."

"I've been to Ogdensburg," Laura offered.

"Oh? Courtney take you there?"

"No. Bert Trebling."

"Ah . . . the solid oak is bending like a willow before charm and beauty," Hannah exclaimed.

"Oh, Hannah." Laura wanted to believe it was the wine that made her face feel so hot and not embarrassment. "It was to see the art works of Remington."

Hannah smiled slyly. "Bert's not the sort of man to do things on impulse. You can be sure he had a definite purpose in taking you there. He's not like our young friend Courtney, who likes the company of pretty women and is a perennial pursuer of such. No. I have the feeling when Bert seeks the company of a woman he has serious designs on her."

Laura had no response. Her mind spun with hazed thoughts about the two men who had just entered her life and aroused sensations of a past she wanted to forget. Peter, Kevin and Bert mingled and diffused in her mind, becoming one entity then dispersing into separate niches in her brain.

"Ah, here we are. Safe and sound," said Hannah, pulling in an oar as the boat bumped against the dock. Laura reached out and yanked the back of the boat close to the dock and hopped out.

"Thanks for everything, Hannah."

"It's only the beginning, my dear. Only the beginning."

Puzzled by her parting words, Laura stood on the dock and watched the regal form row back out into the river, her heart filled with a genuine fondness for the idiosyncratic woman.

She sighed heavily as the boat dimmed in her view. She turned and faced the brooding mansion and with measured steps started up the incline to the house.

Her concentration on work was so weak, her ear was more attuned to her little radio. When the announcer of the program stated the next hour of uninterrupted music would be devoted to the waltzes of Johann Strauss, a melancholy elation surged through her as she thought of the tall, dark man who had whirled her around in his arms at the old inn.

The wine had weakened her resolve to increase her work effort and let her give in to a desire to dance in the large ballroom downstairs. No one would ever know and it would be an opportunity that might never come her way again. Her foggy mind thought it was all very rational.

She walked down the marble steps, which befit her mood, gracefully, sweeping down the staircase as if she were dressed in a wide rustling gown of the nineteenth century. She knew how Cinderella must have felt.

She carefully closed the foyer doors and placed the radio on one of the marble-topped tables off to the side, then turned up the volume slightly. She swayed to the music for several moments, waiting for it to enter her body and soul completely.

She swirled around the spacious, empty room almost believing she had been transported to another time and another place. When the waltz came to an end, she curtsied, lifting her make-believe brocaded gown of silk to her nonexistent partner.

"Is this a private party or can anyone join?"

Laura spun around, her heart sinking, a hot flush running through her veins. She could feel the arteries in her neck pulsing nervously, her heart thundering in her heaving bosom.

Stunned, she stared at the powerful figure leaning casually against the open door that connected the ballroom to the dining room. Damn! She had forgot to close that one! Bert's muscular arms were folded over his chest and there was a look in his eyes she couldn't fathom. It pierced right through her to settle at the base of her spine, sending trickles of shivers throughout her being. His eyes shifted as they swept her lithe form, making her feel weak and foolish. Why? Why did he have to see me behaving like an idiot? she asked herself over and over, then wished the floor would open up and swallow her.

"I didn't know women these days still knew how to blush," he stated laconically and began to walk toward her.

"There are probably a lot of things you don't know about women, Mr. Trebling," she replied defensively, going to the radio and snapping it off brusquely. The magic moment had fled. She longed to be back on the second floor, safe amid her work.

"I doubt it," he answered coolly, a knowing smile on his face.

"If you'll excuse me, I must get back to work." She grabbed the radio and began her course of escape toward the door.

"I'm quite surprised at you, Miss Bickford. I didn't think you were the sort to leave your work for such frivolous amusements. I always thought you were the dedicated kind, driven to abstraction by overwhelming ambition."

"Look, Mr. Trebling, it is no concern of yours whether I am dedicated or ambitious or not. I won't be here much longer so I suggest we both try to be a little more civil on those few occasions when our paths unwittingly cross. I realize you cannot change your ingrained sarcastic personality overnight and the effort might overtax you; however, on my part, it will be no strain. I was brought up to be polite no matter how trying the circumstances were."

He applauded, the sharp clap echoing through the room, but his smile was diabolical, masking the grimness in his eyes. "You think me brutish? Barbarous?"

"Yes!" she cried and turned her back on him, her feelings torn asunder. A distorted anger was quickly replacing her former embarrassment.

"And I suppose the polished, debonair Kevin Courtney is more to your liking. Ambition to match ambition," he sneered tauntingly.

Slowly she turned to face him, trying to keep her temper in check. "At least he's a civilized gentleman. Furthermore, I don't know what your hang-up is on ambition but there are some people in this world who would find janitoring totally without stimulation to their intellectual capabilities," she hurled back at him vexatiously.

"Ha! Now not only am I crude, but stupid to boot!"

"If the shoe fits, wear it."

As she neared the door, his hand closed around her upper arm, sending shock waves over the surface of her skin.

"You thought me neither stupid nor a brute when we danced together at the inn," he said with a deep softness in his voice that made her dizzy.

She summoned every bit of strength she had and tried to wrench her arm free but his hand held fast. His other broad hand snatched the radio from her and put it back on the side table, taking her with him. He turned it on and, hearing the strains of the waltz continuing, turned the volume up so loud it reverberated throughout the ballroom.

"Now, Miss Bickford, we shall see just how crude I am." He pulled her to him roughly, staring smugly into her amber eyes, then whirled her off to the lilting rhythms of the Strauss opus.

He danced with an air of gallantry that Laura thought only existed in another age. He swung her around and around the floor, his strong arms steady and sure. At first she tried to resist him but his commanding manner and brute strength precluded any escape and she finally relaxed, letting her illusions take over once again. She began to pray the music would never end. But it did and she found herself sheepishly looking up at him. He smiled down at her, crookedly and without a trace of the usual mockery, creating a turbulence in her brain she didn't know how to cope with.

"Am I so bad?" he asked softly, stopping in the dance but keeping his grip on her.

"I don't know. You confuse me," she whispered hesitantly.

"What kind of woman are you, Miss Bickford?"

"Like any other, I suppose."

"The career comes first, everything else is secondary?"

"Sometimes it is a necessity."

"Is it now? Haven't you ever been in love, Miss Bickford?"

"You're getting personal, Mr. Trebling. I think it's time for me to leave. Thank you for the dance."

"Ah! 'Tales from the Vienna Woods'! I never could resist that one." He tightened his hold on her and once again swept her out onto the empty marble floor. His stamina far surpassed hers as he whirled her about until the waltz came to a conclusion.

Breathless and speechless, Laura leaned against him, unconscious of her spontaneous reaction. His arms enveloped her, drawing her to his hard unyielding body. Numb with weariness and the effects of the wine, she offered no resistance. She felt his lips brush against her hair but then thought that her state of exhaustion had induced an overactive imagination. She lifted her head from his heaving chest and gazed into his startling blue eyes.

"Really, Mr. Trebling, I must do some work."

He pressed her closer. "Must you?" His voice was deep and oddly husky while his eyelids drooped seductively.

Her glance fixed on his widely parted lips that were coming down to claim hers. She squirmed in his arms and brought her splayed hands to his broad chest.

"No," she pleaded as his lips brushed against hers.

"Why not?" His breath mingled with hers while his mouth teased the outer edges of her lips, causing her to forget any rational objection that might halt the rapacious assault. And did she really want him to stop?

Her hands pushed against his expansive chest and she opened her mouth to insist he release her instantly when he effectively silenced her by hungrily covering her mouth with his own. The kiss excited her to a pitch where her blood raced hot in scattering directions. Her legs weakened, grazing the taut muscles of his thighs, while the pressure of her hands abruptly ceased. She let them slide over his chest to the heavy muscles of his shoulders and before she could stop them, they were around his neck insisting his head remain in contact with hers. The kiss deepened and widened with such turbulence and anxiety, the music in the background sounded like an echo chamber pulsing in rhythm to their undulating mouths, which seemed intent on consuming one another.

Unashamed, she clung to him, delight curling low in her abdomen as his lips sought the tender spots along her neck. A jubilant bliss soared through her as her hands pressed hard against his back.

"Are you aware of what you are doing to me, Miss Bickford?" he asked softly, his lips fanning her ear with his words.

"No," she whispered, almost incapable of speech. Between his lips taunting her skin, his after-shave delighting her nostrils and the entrancing music flooding the ballroom, her senses were shattered and strewn about like shards of a precious vase. She was fearful that she might awaken at any minute to find she was still alone in the great ballroom and that it was only her imagination that had run wild. She let her fingers roam over the thick cords of his neck to assure herself he was really there and holding her.

"You're slowly tearing me apart. I don't know how much longer I can take it," he rasped hoarsely as his lips sped across her cheek to once again seek the solace of her mouth with lingering ardor.

When his kiss began to border on unbridled urgency, a clarifying flame burst within her and reason came crashing in around her, bringing her back to reality and earth.

Once again she brought her hands to press against his chest and free her lips from his.

"Let me go!" she demanded.

"Why?" he asked, his voice thick and husky as his half-opened and glazed blue eyes scanned her face with desire.

"I have work to do."

"It can wait."

"No, it can't." She stiffened under his hands, steeling herself to be firm and break the spell he was casting over her with increasing power.

"There's always tomorrow," he suggested, his eyes glistening and his lips starting a downward course toward hers.

"I don't believe in procrastination. I've wasted enough time and I don't intend to waste any more here with you," she said icily. The words escaped her lips before her heart had a chance to temper them.

As if she had thrown a pail of ice water in his face, Bert released her and stepped back proffering a mocking bow.

"Of course, Miss Bickford." His face took on the essence of chipped ice and a haughty coolness invaded his eyes. "Your time is much too valuable to be wasted on a lowly caretaker. I had forgotten how ambition can obliterate the human aspect of life. Never let it be said that a mere janitor such as I ever stood in the way of your success." A bitter smile widened on his lips as his eyes searched hers with probing intensity before he turned and left the ballroom.

She stood there blinking back the tears that were beginning to swell in the corners of her eyes as the small radio persisted in playing another Strauss waltz. She ran across the marble floor and quickly snapped it off, thinking if she never heard another waltz again it would be too soon.

Clutching the radio with the same tenacity with which she held the vision of what had just occurred, she dragged herself up the main staircase to the second floor with reluctance.

She absently glanced about her papers, the paintings on the easels, the floodlights in place, and wondered if she'd ever find the impetus to work as she had done when she first arrived on the island.

Idly, she traced a finger over the frame of one of the paintings. At least she now knew Bert was aware of her as a woman. He did express a certain feeling for her even though the word *love* was never mentioned. Her tenure on the island would soon be over and, though she would leave behind priceless art treasures, she would take memories that would last a lifetime.

The anguish of departing vanished, leaving in its stead an incentive to finish the job quickly and efficiently. It would be foolish for her to torture herself by lingering in the mansion to be near a man whom she knew she would never see again. Over the next few days, she would photograph the few remaining treasures and that would be the end of her stay at Evans Mansion and the Thousand Islands.

CHAPTER 7

Laura's sleep was invaded by surrealistic dreams. She saw herself in a huge ballroom whose ceiling was the open sky. Peter's arms were around her, spinning her across the room. She looked at him and his face slowly changed to that of Kevin. Then she saw Peter standing at the end of the ballroom, an amused smile on his face, when he suddenly vanished and she was dancing alone surrounded by tall, formally attired men, every one of them the image of Bert, the caretaker, and all smiling at her sardonically. She stopped dancing and stood trembling as the imposing figures tightened their circle, closing in on her. She awoke with a start as the dream darkened.

The now-familiar motel room was a welcome sight. The dream had left her shaken, for it all seemed so real, so vivid. It had been a long time since she had dreamed about Peter and she wondered why she had now. Was she still in love with him? Or think she was? Or was she trying to project her former feeling for him onto Kevin? And what did Bert Trebling have to do with either of them?

She smiled to herself for letting a silly dream affect her like that. But it did help to reinforce her determination not to become emotionally involved with any man. She had a promising future ahead of her and could well afford to be independent.

The next two days passed uneventfully and time slipped by with astonishing speed. Laura calculated her work would be finished in the next day or so and she could head back to Brooklyn.

It was a gloomy day and the threat of a storm was ominously present. As she walked to the restaurant, the heavy dampness in the air caused her hair to spring into ringlets around her face. This would be her last day on the island. Tomorrow morning she would be on her way back to the city at last. Her step lightened and her gait quickened. She hoped the clouds would disperse and the day turn pleasant, for she wanted to have a last walk around the island. She didn't know when or if she'd ever be in the area again and wanted to emblazon her mind with every detail of the place.

She was disappointed to see Sam at the helm of the boat when she

84 *Invitation to a Waltz*

reached the dock. She was certain Kevin knew it was her last day in Alexandria Bay but, she shrugged, maybe he was waiting for the return trip so they could spend the evening together.

Sam appeared unusually moody as they headed out into the river. "Something wrong, Sam?" she asked.

"I don't like it," he said, shaking his head. "Not at all. Maybe we'd better head back, miss. I think you ought to stay in town today."

"Whatever for?"

"The clouds are gettin' thick in a way I don't like. We're in for a real bad one, we are. Why don't I just turn around and take you back to the dock?"

"Nonsense, Sam. I'll be finished today and I'm not about to let a little storm stop me." Then she added, "Nor a big one either."

"As you say, miss. But don't say I didn't warn you." Sam's countenance grew grave as he narrowed his eyes and peered at the swelling waters of the river. It was almost as if they were speaking to him and their words were filled with foreboding. Laura was amused by the way the old man kept shaking his head all the way to the island.

Bert was leaning against the dock post casually as they pulled up. "Take her back, Sam," he ordered gruffly.

"You'll do no such thing, Sam," she said, climbing out of the boat.

Bert gripped her arm with such force she thought she would tumble back into the boat. "Get back in there," he growled.

"I certainly will not!" she snapped back at him. "And let go of my arm. You're not my keeper."

"Well, somebody should be." He loosened his hold a bit but did not relinquish her arm. "Listen to me, Miss Bickford, you've never seen the force with which a storm can hit around here. At times it's frightening." His voice was stern but a little gentler.

"I'm not afraid of thunderstorms, Mr. Trebling. You have no need to worry on my account."

"Go back with Sam," he warned, a pleading urgency flaring from the depths of his usually placid blue eyes.

"I will not."

"He's right, miss. I should have refused to bring you over when I saw the sky." Sam looked worried and sheepish at the same time.

Bert started to nudge her back into the boat when she wrenched free of him, anger blazing in her amber eyes.

"I will not be bullied, least of all by you, Mr. Trebling. I'll be finished here today and you need never concern yourself with me again. This is my last trip here and I'm going to complete my work here today whether you like it or not." Laura stalked off in the direction of the mansion, leaving Sam shaking his head dolefully and Bert yelling after her in frustration.

"I didn't think you were witless enough to let ambition rule out good sense."

Laura turned in fury. "You . . . you . . . you have neither sense nor ambition. You're a perennial beachcomber with no thought of anyone but yourself." She ran to the mansion steps and disappeared inside, ashamed of her outburst.

Sam was still shaking his head when Bert said to him, "Women! You may as well go, Sam. I doubt if I can talk any sense into her at this stage of the game."

Laura slammed the door behind her and raced up the stairs to the second floor. The nerve of that man! Telling her what she could or could not do. She wasn't a child. Why should she let a little storm delay her departure from Evans Mansion? The sooner Bert Trebling was out of her life, the sooner she could return to normal. Though saddened by the thought of not seeing him again, she knew it was for the best.

She took the necessary remaining photographs and packed her equipment. It was almost two in the afternoon and she had forgotten to eat any lunch. She took the thermos out along with a sandwich from her satchel and started to eat while she worked on the written descriptions of the articles she had just photographed, making sure she correctly noted the exact location in the mansion of each item.

She rubbed the back of her neck and leaned back in the chair. Her whole body had begun to stiffen from her cramped position at the table. Standing up and giving her muscles a good stretch, she walked over to the window. She looked up at the sooty sky and saw the clouds churning, their color turning from deep gray to inky black. Even the tops of the trees were starting to bend under the force of the wind.

Now was as good a time as any to take that walk around the island before the rain started, she thought. She could finish the few remaining notes while it was raining and still have plenty of time to clear everything up before the boat came for her at six o'clock.

She threw her sweater over her shoulders and went outside, where the threatening weather had become more aggressive than she had supposed. Some of the gusts of wind were so strong she had to find something to hold on to occasionally to keep from losing her balance.

The sound of pounding water resounded all around her. It was a kind of primordial cadence Laura had never heard before and it fascinated her. She made her way down to the water's edge and mar-

veled at the sight of the frenzied waters lashing against the rocks in
angry futility. She had never seen such high waves on a river before.
She walked along the perimeter, enthralled by the ferocity of the
river, almost hypnotized by it.

She pushed her blowing hair from her face and held it there so she
could see the powerhouse not too far in front of her.

She started to head for it but stopped short when she saw Bert
come around the corner of the stone building clad only in his old cut-
off jeans.

She watched the sinews of his bronzed body ripple and contract as
he carried more crates into the powerhouse. The raw power of his
physique made her tremble and blush. Her heart raced and she knew
she had to get away from him before he saw her there. She couldn't
confront him with any logical thought, for her mind was now in a
turmoil.

She turned and cut crossways over the island. Realizing the boathouse was just ahead, she decided to have a final look at the gargan-
tuan edifice, then return to the house. She smiled at the sight of the
little bridge that the caretaker had so brazenly carried her across. She
walked to the middle of it and, resting her arms on the wooden railing, watched the turbulent waters below. She stared distractedly before realizing there was something different about the water, something she couldn't quite put her finger on at the moment. Then it
dawned on her that the water was higher, much higher, and rapidly
getting higher all the time. It was beginning to swirl over the base of
the bridge. Slow panic crept over her as she watched the waters begin
to rise with increasing speed and envisioned her fall into the tumultu-
ous liquid below if for some reason the bridge collapsed.

She turned swiftly, but as she did her ankle twisted and she slipped
on the slimy stone footings glistening from the rising waters. Her balance gone, she fell, vainly trying to reach the railing. The water
soaked and chilled her from the waist down, her upper torso landing
where the bridge had not yet felt the effect of the lashing waters. The
sudden onslaught of a drenching rain soon had Laura soaked from
head to toe. Her efforts to stand on her foot seemed endless and
fruitless. Her fast-swelling ankle didn't want to cooperate.

She was trying to pull herself up by clutching the supporting legs
of the railing when miraculously she was floating in air in the strong
naked arms of the caretaker while the rain poured down with increasing vengeance.

"You stupid little fool! What the hell are you doing out here?
Can't you see what the weather is like?"

This time Laura had no smart remark to make. He was right. It was foolish of her to come out knowing the weather was inclement. But she felt secure in his arms as the beat of his heart forced her own into the same cadence. Shyly she slipped her arm around his neck as his long legs made their way back to the mansion.

His flesh was scorching her in spite of the cool rain. She felt a delirious pleasure as her hand rested on the thick cords of his neck while shivers of bliss convulsed her. The sensations were novel and unique, beyond any previous experience. Pellets of rain washed over her face and body but could not put out the flames rising within her. She was afraid to look at him for fear he would return that look and she would be lost, reduced to a trembling schoolgirl.

Once inside the house, he set her on her feet only to catch her as her ankle gave way beneath her.

"Why didn't you go back to the mainland when you had the chance?" he asked, then with a sigh of annoyance, he picked her up again and carried her into the library, where he proceeded to get a fire going in the fireplace.

"I'm sorry to have been a bother to you," said Laura shivering, her teeth chattering.

"Start getting out of those wet things while I go upstairs and get something dry for you to put on."

She started with her shoes and stockings as Bert disappeared up the stairs.

"Aren't you out of those wet things yet?" he asked angrily, seeing she had only removed her shoes, stockings and sweater when he entered the room.

"I couldn't very well stand around here naked," she replied, noticing he had put on some dry pants but neglected to put on a dry shirt as well.

"Here . . . get into this," he demanded, thrusting a huge terry cloth robe at her.

"Do you mind?"

"Mind what?"

"Mind leaving the room."

"Oh, for God's sake, woman! You can't be so naïve as to think I've never seen a naked woman before."

"Well, this is one naked woman you're not going to see," she replied testily.

He sighed in exasperation but walked out into the entry hall.

"Please close the door," she called out after him.

He slammed the door shut with a force that echoed throughout the house. Laura removed her wet things as quickly as possible, thinking he might burst in on her at any moment just to be spiteful. She wrapped herself in the fleecy warmth of the robe. Then, making sure the robe exposed no part of her naked form, she told him he could come in. When he reentered the library, she was placing her things as close to the fire as she dared, hobbling about on the swollen foot.

"Oh, sit down, will you? I'll do that." He took her things from her and continued to place them advantageously around the fireplace to receive its warming air.

Laura sat down in the leather armchair, placed her foot on the ottoman in front of it and stared at it with disgust for her own clumsiness. Bert turned and watched her for a moment, then started to leave the room.

"Where are you going?" she asked nervously.

"To get something to bind that foot of yours." He looked at her as though she was a misbehaving child who should be punished in some way, then stalked out of the library.

She gazed unseeing at the fire and shuddered involuntarily as her skin remembered the touch of his flesh on hers, of the massive furred chest where black hair curled tightly as the rain poured over it. She clutched the arms of the chair, trying to will the flutterings in her heart to cease, to leave her alone and not conjure up yearnings that could never be. Tomorrow she would be gone and never see the man again.

Her tender musings were shattered by a horrendous roar of thunder rattling through the room, making her jump in her seat unwittingly. In the city, thunder and lightning had no effect on her and she couldn't remember it ever frightening her as a child in Vermont. For some reason here on the island its portent seemed ominous.

Bert returned with a roll of bandage and knelt down by the ottoman. With a gentleness his big, rough hands belied, he carefully wrapped her ankle snugly with just the right amount of tension. Laura had to check a rising impulse to reach out and stroke the beads of water still clinging to the bent head in front of her.

Finished, he rose and towered above her with a strange glow glinting in those stark blue eyes. With one encompassing glance, Laura took in the man before her, then quickly lowered her eyes to her lap. The sight of his bared, muscled chest was too heady for her. It only started her insides on the road to instability again and right now she needed all her wits about her.

"Perhaps now you can understand why I wanted you to return to the mainland," he growled at her. "Like you, I don't have time to waste either."

She knew she deserved that. Turning her soft amber eyes at him, she said, "I'm truly sorry to have inconvenienced you and I mean that. I doubt if my clothes will be dry by the time the boat comes for me. Would it be too much trouble if I kept the robe until I get back to the motel? I'll make sure it is properly cleaned and leave it at the motel for you." She looked at him wistfully, wanting to apologize for her harsh words when they last met. She hadn't meant to belittle him. But she was afraid an apology would only infuriate him further, making him think she was trying to make a fool of him again.

"The robe is of no consequence, Miss Bickford. If you weren't so foolish, you'd realize there will be no boat to take you back to the mainland until after the storm is over, which probably won't be until tomorrow morning."

"Morning?" asked Laura incredulously. "I can't stay here all night."

"I'm afraid you don't have much choice."

She hopped to the window only to find a rapidly darkening sky. The rain was pelting down in torrents while, now and then, the sky blazed with lightning that left a roaring boom in its wake. In the dim light she could see the trees bending deep in subservience to the wrath of the storm. She turned to Bert, a mixture of fear and perplexity on her pallid face.

"But I can't stay here all night," she repeated, entreaty and terror mingling in her shaky voice.

"As I said before, it's not up to you." Bert went to the fire and, poking at it, caused it to leap and sparkle in the dim room. "Why don't you turn on a light?"

As if in a trance, she complied. The light gave her some assurance and comfort.

"I suppose you're right. I may as well make the best of it. I can rework some of my notes."

"Always thinking of work, aren't you? What are you bucking for? Head curator? Or perhaps a cushier job at the Metropolitan Museum of Art?" he inquired snidely.

"Oh, you cretin! You have a narrow, abbreviated, telescopic mind. If I could have something other than an argumentative conversation with you, I might consider putting my work aside and have a nice friendly chat. But knowing you, you would twist whatever I said to suit your warped mind. Under the circumstances, I prefer the solitude of paper work, so if you'll excuse me."

Laura drew her robe around her and, with a regal toss of her head, brushed past him bobbing her way to the desk when suddenly the lights went out. Only the warm glow of the fire cast its shadowy light around the room.

She stood rooted to the spot. "What happened?"

"The generator has finally blown, more than likely," he replied calmly, his hands braced on the back of a Queen Anne chair. The firelight played eerily behind him, illuminating his large frame and rendering him a satanic, foreboding figure. "Those high-powered lights of yours have been putting quite a strain on it. I'm only surprised it hasn't given out long before this."

"I might have known you'd find some way to put the blame on me!" she cried indignantly.

Bert laughed loudly. "You are a touchy little minx, aren't you? The generator is old and more or less held together with chewing gum. It really was never up to handling those lights of yours." Catching her eyes with his, his look became serious, almost glum. "I'll go get the flashlight and see if I can find some oil lamps. One of them should give you enough light to work by."

With a troubled sigh, Bert went in search of the lamps. Laura walked over to the chair where he had been standing and slumped down in it wearily. Her heart was pumping erratically at the thought of being alone with the caretaker for the entire night. Would she have the strength to deny him if he took her in his arms and kissed her? She would have to dredge up every atom of resistance in her being or she would be lost.

She turned her mind from the disturbing notion and forced her brain to concentrate on the wonderful works of Remington she had seen on the day Bert took her downriver to Ogdensburg. Her fine brows knitted together as the image of Bert kept superimposing itself on the Remington paintings. She rose from the chair to spread her hands before the fire, hoping to divert her thoughts and bring them back to the situation at hand as she put all her weight on her good ankle.

She was glad to see the two oil lamps in Bert's hands when he returned. She could work and wouldn't have to be alone with her thoughts. Since she'd moved all her things downstairs in preparation for her departure, it didn't take long for her to spread the necessary papers on the desk.

Bert sprawled in a chair by the fire, opposite her. He casually threw his long leg over the arm of the chair and clasped his hands together, his index fingers forming a steeple, which he gently brushed over his lips as he stared at Laura.

She felt his searing gaze on her even though she pretended to be deeply engrossed in her work. But his stare was starting to grate on her nerves to the point where she could neither think nor concentrate.

"And just what do you find so fascinating here?" she asked, her irritation plainly showing.

"Is my presence annoying you? I thought you were so wrapped up in your work you didn't even know I existed." His mouth was twisted in a mocking smile, taunting her with a knowing look in his stormy blue eyes. "Shall I leave the warmth of the fire and the pleasure of your delightful and stimulating company?" His sarcasm was more than evident.

"What you do is no concern of mine." Laura returned his glance but dropped her eyes quickly. Those blue eyes of his seemed to penetrate her very soul.

"Then I shall stay where it is cozy."

Laura's handwriting was slowly turning into a nervous scribble. The thought of him sitting there watching her every move was reducing her to a mass of quivering jelly.

The sound of thunder crashed into the silent room as if to remind its occupants of its existence. Rain came down like slicing sheets of glass, thudding against the house, cutting on the window panes. The wind picked up, making mournful pleas as it swept past the mansion. Mother Nature's torturous calls lured Laura to the window. She peered out into the darkened world not really knowing what she expected to see. She stiffened as she felt the warmth of another body behind her.

"There is nothing more awesome than nature when it is at odds with itself," murmured Bert, standing close to her.

"I find it beautiful in a frightening sort of way," she replied, looking straight ahead into the darkness, trying not to think of the hands that were being placed on her shoulders.

One hand lifted to gently brush her hair aside. All perception of reality drained from her as Bert's warm lips began to scorch her neck. Her flesh tingled as the sensation ran through her whole being. His large, rough hands turned her around slowly. She couldn't hide the anxiety on her face nor the questions in her eyes.

Then his eyes met hers, not with the usual malicious arrogance, but with a soft, tender and growing hunger. There was an unreasonable anguish flashing in her eyes as he took her small head between his powerful hands and lowered his mouth to hers with an air of undeniable authority.

Laura fought her own desire to respond to him and let him vent whatever passions he may have had for her. But she knew she had to master the situation at once or she would be at his mercy as she struggled to smother her own urges. She braced her hands against his furred chest, her fingers burning at the touch of his bare flesh, and pushed herself away from him with all the strength she could command. The storm had isolated them and she knew there was no place to hide, no six o'clock boat.

The surprise at being repulsed that registered on Bert's face was quickly replaced by a confident and determined smile. "You don't think you're going to get away from me that easily, do you?" he asked as his sinewy arm encircled her tiny waist with steely resolution and drew her to him with unbridled force.

She was completely powerless and defenseless in the face of his overwhelming strength. He could, and she thought he would, control her at his whim. A tremor ran through her as his head bent down to hers once again. His mouth, hard and purposeful, demanded a response. It was with reluctance she tried to free herself and, in a way, she was grateful he held her fast. His lips became more and more insistent, more forceful, until the increased pressure compelled her lips to part.

Her hesitation was brief, fleeting, before she responded with a passion and a hunger that came raging forth and went beyond her conscious control. The impact of his lips merging so gently and lovingly with hers made her reel and her body automatically leaned into his. She could feel the tension in him growing as the kiss deepened and widened. They clung to one another, lost in a private world. The air crystallized around them and the room vulcanized under the pressure of intensifying emotions.

Suddenly, with frightening clarity, Laura knew she belonged to this strange man. Never again would she experience this feeling of total oneness with any other man. Peter and Kevin became dim shadows in a vague dream, dancers in a tuneless waltz.

The kiss ended, leaving them both shaken by desires neither had realized the depth of. Laura nestled her head in his broad shoulder while he held her tightly and stroked her hair fondly. No words were spoken, none were needed.

The storm outside raged and howled savagely but couldn't begin to match the turbulence boiling within the two people alone in Evans Mansion.

For the first time in her life, Laura lost all sense of propriety, all sense of self-preservation. This caretaker had become the only motivating force in her life.

His hand lovingly cupped her chin and their lips found solace in renewed exploration. The flesh of his taut leg muscles brushed her bare leg as her robe fell slightly open. A convulsive shudder sped through her and, unconsciously, she clung to him with growing ardor and the room became charged with an electrical force greater than the bolts of lightning slashing through the air outside.

As the heat from his body flowed into hers with increasing rapidity, she became aware of the dangerous position she was slipping into even though she didn't want the moment to end. Instinctively she knew their passions were fast reaching the point of no return as his hands traveled over her slim body, making the skin under her robe come alive with an aching hunger. As his lips moved to kiss each of her quivering eyelids before returning to ravish her mouth once again, she didn't know how much longer she would be able to maintain a vestige of willpower. It wouldn't be much longer before their fevered emotions would erupt as violently as the storm outside. She couldn't delude herself any longer; she had to break away from him before it was too late. Solidifying her willpower, she twisted free of his arms and free of his lips, then quickly limped to the overstuffed chair by the fireplace, putting her hands on its high back.

Before her lungs could swallow the air they needed, Bert was in back of her, his hands gently kneading the muscles between her neck and shoulders.

"What is it?" he asked softly.

She shook her head ruefully. "This whole situation is impossible, Mr. Trebling. I don't know what got into me. I never should have let it happen in the first place."

"Do I repulse you?" he asked, his hands becoming motionless on her shoulders as if dreading the reply. Again she shook her head. "Well . . . then . . ." He gripped her shoulders in an effort to spin her around but she remained rigidly immobile. His hands quickly dropped to his sides and he moved away from her. "I suppose the charms of Kevin Courtney are more to your liking. After all, he's an up and coming young designer while I'm only a caretaker with no burning ambition. Isn't that what you said? A beachcomber I believe the word was. However, I assure you, Miss Bickford, even a beachcomber can have desires." His tone was low and seductive.

As Laura spun to face him, she caught the painful glint in his eyes as he ran a shaky hand through his thick black hair. She wanted to laugh at his suggestion that she would prefer Kevin to him but had to maintain her air of indifference if she was to survive the night intact.

"Your desires are no concern of mine and I would prefer to be alone, if you don't mind." She brought her eyes to meet his with a courage she didn't truly possess as she drew the robe around her and yanked the cord with a spiteful jerk.

"Those big calf eyes of yours are denying your words, Miss Bickford." He began to close the gap between them. She gingerly stepped back, a look of bewildered anxiety creeping across her face and into her eyes.

"Get out of here," she whispered hoarsely.

"By what right do you think you can dismiss me? You're the interloper here," he said, gaining a measure of control over his passions.

"Mr. Trebling, I find your behavior ungentlemanly. It would be base of you to take advantage of our isolation here. I think it would be best if you retired to your quarters for both our sakes," she suggested, trying to still the quake in her voice.

"Do you now?" His eyes were laughing at her daringly as he took another step toward her, his handsome, sharp-boned face enhanced by the flickering light of the fire.

She moved back farther, knowing if he so much as touched her again she would melt in his arms, throwing all caution to the wind. Oh, how she wanted to be in those strong arms again and have his fiery kisses burn her lips. She had to forcibly drain her body of its emotional tide. She took a few more steps away from him and, feeling the fireplace rack by her foot, reached down behind her. Her fingers wrapped convulsively around the iron poker.

"If you take one step closer, I'll use this," she threatened, brandishing the poker in her hand and feeling like a misbegotten heroine out of a gothic novel.

"The first time I saw you you were waving a poker about. I suppose it is only fitting you should do the same on our last evening together." He looked down at her indulgently, as if she were a small child flirting with defiance for the first time.

Laura bit her lower lip but never lowered her gaze as she watched Bert's eyes appraise her. He visually drank deep of her, like a man who had known hunger and was storing enough food for the lean times ahead.

"I wonder if you are really capable of using that thing," he taunted and edged closer.

"Try me and see," she warned, raising the poker higher and hating the man for exposing her vulnerability to his touch.

"I do believe you would, Miss Bickford," he laughed, then feigned a yawn. "If you'll excuse me, the hour grows late and I must take my leave of you. Unless, of course, you'd care to join me." There was a trace of whimsy in his voice but Laura only saw the solemn fire in his eyes.

"You must be mad to think I'd go anywhere with you. And it's absolutely barbarous for you to even suggest such a thing. I'd swim to the mainland before I'd let you so much as come near me—ever again."

"How inconsistent is the female species!"

"No more so than their male counterpart," she said with vehemence, truly astonished by his reversal of moods.

He gave her a quick sardonic smile, bowed from the waist while flourishing one hand in the air and left the room.

He is crazy, she thought, and I must be mad too even to be thinking about him. Why did I let him see how I felt about him? She let the poker drop back in the stand and absently put a few more logs on the fire. She pushed the ottoman close to the large overstuffed chair and settled down into it, hoping sleep would obliterate her senses and thoughts. The flickering fire, blazing in shades of red, orange, yellow and blue, mesmerized her. She didn't know how long she sat there staring into the fire trying to dull her overactive mind.

"Girl? Where are you? Laura? Are you all right? Laura?"

The sharp voice penetrated the void of sleep. Laura blinked slowly, trying to sort everything out. Then she remembered the storm and her confinement on the island.

"I'm in here," she called, rubbing the back of her neck and wishing she had some hot coffee.

"My dear child, are you all right? That was quite a storm we had last night. I knew you'd never make it back to the mainland," stated Hannah Lawson, striding into the library.

"I'm fine, Hannah. A bit stiff from the chair though," groaned Laura as she stirred herself from the chair. She raised her arms above her head and stretched vigorously to ease the tight feeling in her muscles. "What time is it?"

"It's seven in the morning. What a wretched night! I came over to see if you survived it. I also brought a thermos of hot tea for you. It'll start your blood flowing." Hannah unscrewed the top section of the thermos, poured a generous amount of tea into it and handed it to Laura. "You must come back with me and I'll make you a hot, nourishing breakfast."

"I appreciate the offer, Hannah, but I'm finished here and will be heading back to the city today." She took a full swallow of the hot liquid and found it refreshing. "This is excellent!"

"I'll make a tea drinker of you yet. It's what I call my morning tea. A mixture of herbs and tea. Spearmint, orange mint, lemon balm, some oolong and Ceylon teas. The teas are fresh, not that commercial stuff which, more than likely, has sat on some shelf for eons. I know an importer who sees to it I have fresh teas from the Orient."

"It certainly makes a difference. You're right, I could become a tea addict."

"It's easily obtained in the city. I'll give you the name and address of the place to go. Tell him I sent you, then he won't try and palm off any stale stuff on you."

While Hannah scribbled down the location of the vendor, Laura got into her dry but wrinkled clothes and left the robe draped over the back of a chair, touching it with a devotion she knew was hopeless. She wondered if he would be down to say good-bye but had a sinking feeling in her heart when she realized he wouldn't. He was not that gracious.

"My address and telephone number are on the paper also. I'll be there around the first of September and I fully expect you to get in touch with me. Well, now that you're dressed, shall I help you carry your paraphernalia down to the dock? It's a beautiful morning outside. As the saying goes, the calm after the storm."

Laura took the paper from Hannah, then drained the rest of the tea from the cap of the thermos. "I'm ready whenever you are, Hannah. I must say I'm not sorry to go."

"Oh? You've had a change of heart?" Hannah stared at her quizzically for a moment, then continued, "Could the dashing Bert Trebling have anything to do with your new attitude? After all, you did spend the night on the island alone with him."

"Hardly," fibbed Laura, knowing the old woman could see right through her, as her cheeks reddened at the very mention of his name.

"Well, I certainly wouldn't blame you in the least, child. He has a way of setting this old blood to boiling on occasion."

Hannah picked up some of the tripods and stands while Laura collected the rest of the equipment. Between them, they managed to get everything into their arms.

Between Hannah's chatter and concentrating on getting down the incline without falling or dropping anything as she hobbled behind Hannah on her sore ankle, she didn't notice the brooding caretaker high on the balcony watching her leave.

Kevin was tying up the boat as they reached the dock. He looked up as they approached and rushed to help them.

"Sorry, Laura. It was impossible to pick you up last night. I hope the night here wasn't too awful for you." His face displayed an apologetic concern.

"I understand, Kevin. No need for apologies."

"She's here, safe and sound and none the worse for wear," stated Hannah matter-of-factly.

Silently Kevin loaded Laura's things into the boat while the two women confronted each other.

"Don't forget me now, Laura," said Hannah with a sadness in her voice she made no attempt to hide.

"I won't," said Laura and kissed the older woman on the cheek. "I could never forget you, Hannah. I'll be looking forward to our reunion in the city this fall."

She got into the boat and, as Kevin revved the engines and headed for the mainland, waved her hand even when Hannah was no more than a blur in the background.

Kevin walked Laura back to the motel and helped her carry the gear.

"I wish you didn't have to leave," he said as she opened the trunk of her VW. "Couldn't you tell your boss you're taking some vacation time? The season is only just beginning here. There are so many things we could do and see."

Laura laughed, her amber eyes sparkling in the early morning light as she began to cram her things into the VW's storage space.

"I'll have to admit it's a pleasant and tempting thought, but one I couldn't seriously entertain. All this material I've been working on has to be typed and the photographs have to be developed for presentation to the insurance company. I do have a deadline, you know."

"You leave me no choice. I shall have to come to the city," he said and smiled.

"Would you mind trying to get the rest of this gear into the car while I get my things from the room and settle my bill at the office?" asked Laura, ignoring his prior statement. She wanted no commitments, no promises that might not be kept by either of them.

While in the room, she quickly washed her face and changed into a skirt and blouse that weren't quite so wrinkled. She brushed her hair and applied some light makeup. With a sigh, she picked up her two suitcases and looked around to make sure she hadn't left anything behind. Feeling a little neater, she paid her bill and headed for the car, where Kevin was waiting for her.

"You're a quick-change artist if I ever saw one," he said, taking the suitcases from her. He put one in the trunk then slammed it shut before placing the other one on the back seat of the car. When he backed out of the cramped little car, he took her hands in his.

Seeing the look in his eyes she knew he was about to kiss her. She couldn't bear it; her lips still burned from Bert's ardent kisses. She had the silly notion she never again wanted to feel anyone's lips but his on hers again. She gave Kevin a swift kiss on the cheek and slipped into the car, pulling the door shut behind her.

He stooped down to speak to her as she rolled the window down. "Must you really go?" he pleaded.

"Yes. I must. It's a long drive and I don't relish arriving in the city too late at night."

"We'll meet again, Laura. I'll see to it." He ran his hand through his unruly sandy hair.

"Good-bye, Kevin. And thanks for everything."

"Never say good-bye, Laura," he called as she started the engine and whirled the little car out of the motel's courtyard.

She headed for the New York Thruway as if all the demons in hell were after her. There was an urgency, a need in her to get as far away from Evans Mansion as possible, as if the distance would expunge all memories of the mansion and its caretaker from her brain.

Tears welled in her eyes, blurring the highway before her, as the love she felt for the irascible caretaker overpowered her. Kevin and Peter receded from her mind like the remnants of a sandy shore getting washed away by the ebb tide.

CHAPTER 8

"The photographs were superb, Laura! The insurance company is very pleased with the work you did. I even hear Nathaniel Harte was satisfied. Being an artist, he can be a very difficult man." The small balding man wrung his hands anxiously while small beads of perspiration glistened on his forehead like morning dew. "I want to commend you personally for the job you did for the museum."

Laura was floating on air from the profusion of compliments she had received that morning but the enthusiasm shown by Mr. Donaldson was especially exhilarating.

"Thank you, Mr. Donaldson."

"Don't thank me. I want to thank you. Because of your efforts, Mr. Harte has agreed to show his works here at our museum. Do you realize what a coup that will be? The very thought of a Harte exhibition sends shivers down my spine. More importantly, he has consented to attend a private preexhibition showing the evening before it is open to the public. Imagine! The cream of the New York art world here at this museum." John Donaldson's eyes almost whirled in his head at the thought. Laura had to smother a growing tendency to giggle.

"Has he set any specific date?" she asked with a pretense at reserve.

"No . . . no . . . I believe he mentioned something about the fall when I talked to him on the phone."

"Oh, is he back from Europe?"

"I don't think so. The call was long distance and there was so much static I could hardly hear him. Can you imagine having him here, in person! He is a very elusive man. Hardly ever makes public appearances and he is very selective in his companions, I understand. And quite the lady's man, although he is seldom seen with the same woman more than once or twice."

Mr. Donaldson surprised Laura. He was not the sort of man who passed along gossip. She chalked it up to his overexcited state of mind. He continued with an accounting of the owners and museums

who would be willing to lend them works not in Mr. Harte's possession, but Laura was no longer listening. Her mind was occupied by
the thoughts of such an exhibit—which rooms would be most suitable, what kind of lighting to use to enhance the paintings. Fall was
still many weeks away so she had plenty of time to work the details
out, that is, if Mr. Donaldson would let her work on it. Her heart
sank at the prospect he wouldn't.

"By the way, Laura, Mr. Harte did mention something about you
being in charge and directing the exhibit. Your work at the Evans
Mansion impressed him greatly," said Mr. Donaldson, removing any
doubts she may have had about the role she would play in the forth-
coming exhibition.

The summer went by quickly and, on most weekends, Laura escaped the humid heat of the city by going to Vermont to visit with
her parents. There, the clear, sweet air, nearby lakes and cool green
grass offered a reprieve from the muggy city.

It had been an unusually warm day for late September. Reaching
her apartment, Laura was looking forward to a nice, long soak in the
tub. She was in the mood to luxuriate, so she sprinkled a generous
amount of bubble bath crystals into the steaming water.

She removed her robe and longingly slipped into the tub and its
refreshing water. Aches melted from her muscles, stiffened joints
once again became flexible. The long, hot day faded from her mind.
The ring of the telephone shattered through the apartment, destroy-
ing the peaceful solitude that had enveloped her.

Shoving her arms through the dry terry cloth robe, she wrapped it
around her wet body and went to answer the persistent ringing.

"Hello?" she called into the instrument testily.

"Laura?"

"Yes."

"It sure doesn't sound like you. Do you know who this is?"

"No. And I'm not in the mood for a game of questions and answers."

"Boy! Is my timing off." The voice hesitated a moment. "This is
Kevin. Remember? Kevin Courtney from Alexandria Bay."

"Kevin!" Her voice lightened. "Is it really you?"

"Of course. I told you I'd see you again even if I had to come to
the city."

"Where are you?"

"In a telephone booth about two blocks from your place. I
thought I'd better call and give you some notice before dropping in
on you unexpectedly."

"I'm glad you did. I was in the tub."

"No wonder you were a little edgy when you answered the phone. Were you getting ready to go out?"

"No."

"Good. I'll be there in ten minutes. Okay?"

"Can you make it twenty minutes so I can get myself together?"

"Whatever my lady wishes."

She flew to complete her toilet and get dressed. She donned a filmy orange dress and was brushing her hair to a gleam when a faint knock sounded at the door.

"Kevin?" she called.

"Yes . . . yes. Open the door."

Laura looked with admiration at the well-remembered handsome man, his arms loaded with two large grocery bags.

"As long as I had twenty minutes to kill I thought I'd do some shopping for our dinner. I hope you can cook." His smile was as infectious as ever.

"I'll give it my best shot," she replied, taking one of the bags from him. "Whatever did you buy? This bag is heavy."

"Whatever struck my fancy. Steak, the makings of a salad, french bread, sundries and two fine bottles of Pinot Cabernet. Do you think we can manage on that?"

"I certainly hope so. It looks like there is enough for an army here."

"Nice place you have here," Kevin commented as his eyes scanned the neat, tastefully decorated apartment.

"I call it home," she called from the small kitchenette. "Would you bring the other bag in here while I dig out some appropriate glasses?"

As he stood beside her in the kitchen, Laura noted he was even more attractive than she remembered, especially in his tight corduroy pants and a jacket that matched his sandy hair, complemented by a dark brown shirt opened at the neck. She also noted that Kevin was highly cognizant of his good looks and knew how to use them to his advantage.

"I've missed you, sweet lady," he murmured, brushing his lips against her neck as he moved behind her.

"What brings you to New York?" she asked, unpacking the groceries and ignoring his amorous advances.

"You, my lovely Laura. Each time I see you, you become more beautiful, more tempting." He continued to nuzzle her neck and slipped his arms around her waist.

"Now . . . tell me the real reason," she persisted, trying to act totally unaffected by his affectionate manner.

He released her and moved away. Leaning on the counter, he studied her intently. "Aside from seeing your lovely face, I'm here to whip up some lucrative contracts and treat myself to the sophistication and dazzle of Manhattan's beauteous women. Of course, you're number one on my list. Your brief visit to Alexandria Bay made me realize there was a part of me that still longed for the bright lights and a quicker pace of life."

"How long have you been in town?" She returned his gaze, noting his deep tan.

"A little over two weeks."

"Two weeks?" she gasped with a smile. And I'm supposed to be number one on his list, she thought to herself, amused by the notion.

"Now . . . now. Don't get me wrong. I wasn't avoiding you or anything. On the contrary, I was dying to get in touch with you but I had places to go and people to see first," he explained with that familiar boyish grin lighting his face. "Not mad at me, are you?"

"Don't be silly, Kevin. What you do is your own business and I appreciate the fact you even remembered me," she stated honestly.

"Don't be so modest. You're not that easy to forget. By the way, how did your work at the old mansion turn out? Was it accepted?"

"It all turned out fine. I don't mean to brag but my boss, the insurance company and the owner, Mr. Harte, were delighted with the results."

"Good for you. I always knew you were a sharp little lady."

"I don't know about that," she laughed, "but I'm very happy with the way everything turned out." She paused. "What have you been doing for the past two weeks?"

"Crawling up and down Wall Street."

"Don't tell me you are going to dabble in the stock market?"

"Dabble with its financiers is more like it. You remember the contract I had in Montreal?" Laura nodded an assent. "Well, she put me onto several prospects on Wall Street who were part-time yachtsmen and might possibly be interested in some of my designs. So . . ." He waved his hands in the air in a gesture of resignation.

"Could your boatyard handle all that business? And it's quite a distance from here to the Thousand Islands."

"My boatyard has enough trouble handling one boat, two at the most. No, I'd have them built on Long Island or in Connecticut, depending on where the customer would house the craft. Of course, I'd supervise the construction. If everything works the way I have it planned, you might have me around for a while."

When they finished their dinner, Kevin took the bottle of wine and two glasses over to the oblong glass coffee table in front of the large beige sofa while Laura cleared away the dishes.

"I must say, Laura, that was delicious."

"I'm glad you enjoyed it. After all, I feel I owe you several meals after the time you showed me in Alexandria Bay. I'm only glad I didn't burn it." She sat down on the sofa next to him and took the glass of wine he was extending to her. "Tell me, how is everyone up there?"

"Oh, Sam's just as stodgy as ever. Sally misses your daily appearance at the restaurant. And I hear old Hannah is in the city now. You ought to get in touch with her, you know. She'd love to hear from you. You are one of the very few people she really took to. I could count on the fingers of one hand the number of people she has had on that island of hers. Fewer than that ever had lunch with her."

"I'll make it a point to call her." She took a sip of the wine and kept her eyes on the red liquid as she asked, "And Mr. Trebling . . . is he still at the mansion?" It was the first time she had said his name aloud since leaving the mansion. Something inside her constricted, causing the fine hairs on her arms to rise.

"As far as I know, he left a couple of days before they opened the place to the public. The mansion has become a real boon to the tourist trade. Shops, restaurants, everywhere . . . packed . . . and with people anxious to spend money. I had to hire on a couple of extra men to meet the demand for shuttle service to the island."

Laura had to bite her tongue to keep from asking where the caretaker went. She wished she had never mentioned it, for now she couldn't get her mind off the man. She hardly heard Kevin telling anecdotes about the tourists.

Her reverie was shattered when she suddenly found herself in Kevin's arms, his mouth coming down hard on hers. Automatic reflexes took control and she pulled away, blatant astonishment on her face.

"What is it, Laura?" asked Kevin, quizzically eyeing her.

"Nothing. I'm afraid it's been a long day."

"It is getting late," he agreed, glancing at his watch. "I suppose I should be going, unless you wish me to spend the night with you?"

"Kevin! How dare you! No man has ever stayed in my apartment overnight. And none ever shall," she cried indignantly.

"Whoa . . . whoa there," laughed Kevin. "I was only teasing you. I knew you weren't that kind of girl when I first met you. You had an unmistakable air of innocence about you." He took her hand in his and kissed it lightly. "Am I forgiven?"

"I think I'm the one who should ask forgiveness. There was no call for me to jump down your throat like that," she said softly, regretting her moody outburst instantly. Everything had been fine until she started to think about that caretaker.

Kevin rose from the sofa and took Laura's hands in his, pulling her to her feet. "I really must be going. I have an early appointment tomorrow and I hope a number of very busy days ahead."

"Thank you for the lovely dinner, Kevin."

"No. It is the cook we must thank. I'll call you. Good night, sweet lady." He kissed her on the cheek tenderly.

She crawled into bed with unsettled feelings invading her mind before she fell asleep only to find the tall, handsome, unfathomable Bert Trebling haunting her dreams.

Laura turned the handle of the highly polished brass doorbell. She took stock of the old brownstone that squatted among the myriad of stone buildings that some gigantic hands had pressed together in a moment of fury. She had never been in this particular section of Manhattan before and found it a totally new experience. At first appearance, when she had started down the street, all the buildings had seemed flat and alike. But standing at the door and looking down the block, she saw it wasn't a constant facade. The buildings undulated, curving in and out like the swell and dip of the ocean. Varying nuances of architectural deviations also became more apparent as she concentrated on their form.

She turned in anticipation as the large mahogany door swung open.

"Miss Bickford?" politely asked the somber-faced older man whose correct attire could only leave one with the distinct knowledge he was the butler.

"Yes."

"Come in, please. Miss Lawson is expecting you. This way, please."

Laura was amazed to find such opulence behind such a grim exterior. The white plastered ceilings were graced with fluted cornices and trailing rosettes that looped to a point at the apex of the foyer's ceiling. The marble floors were polished like mirrors. She followed the butler down the oriental-carpeted hall where he stopped and knocked gently on a richly carved door before swinging it open for her to enter.

"Laura, my dear. I'm so glad you finally called. I'm so happy to see you again," said Hannah, rising from behind a cherry desk whose patina glistened from the filtered sunlight streaming in from the window beside it.

"Hannah, it's so good to see you again. Although, somehow, you don't seem the same person I knew on the island." Laura studied the immaculately groomed woman before her. The graying hair was expertly coiffed, her dress high fashion—sedate and expensive. One did not have to be an expert to know the pearls were real.

"Never let a person's exterior fool you. I'm still the same woman you knew in the islands," said Hannah, giving Laura a warm friendly hug as the women kissed each other's cheek. "Tell me, was your work at the mansion successful?"

"More than I hoped it would be," answered Laura, sitting in the seat Hannah indicated.

"And what does that mean?"

"Mr. Harte was so impressed, he is lending the museum a number of his works for a special showing and I am to be in charge of the exhibit," she replied breathlessly. For some reason she wanted Hannah to be proud of her.

"My congratulations, my dear. I always knew you were something special. Incidentally, I was reading about Mr. Harte in the society column the other day. It mentioned that upon his return to Manhattan a few weeks ago, he has stepped out of character and entered the social whirl with rare gusto, squiring a different young eligible socialite every night. The column went on to say that one of the young ladies is desperately angling to become the only one."

"Isn't he a little old for that?"

"Hardly. I believe he is in his early or mid thirties. It's amazing to find someone that age getting such jubilant praise from the art world. They usually wait until someone is too old to enjoy the fame or, more often than not, when they are dead and beyond the luxuries of wealth. Our Mr. Harte seems to be one of those rare exceptions."

"Have you ever met him?" Laura's curiosity was aroused. She had always imagined Nathaniel Harte to be rather elderly and gaunt, an aging symbol of success. To learn he was so young was intriguing.

"No. I was never a patron of the fine arts. I prefer the opening of the opera and concert seasons to the shows and exhibitions in the world of art. In fact, I have two box seats at Lincoln Center for tonight. Itzhak Perlman is the soloist with the New York Philharmonic. I presume you're free this evening."

"I'm . . . yes . . . I'm free. But I'm certainly not dressed for the occasion. For the balcony, maybe . . . but not box seats."

"I didn't think you would be. I've planned a little shopping trip for us at Bergdorf's before dinner to get you properly outfitted."

"Hannah, on my salary?" Laura laughed. "I couldn't even buy a lipstick at Bergdorf's."

"Who said anything about you paying?"

"Oh, Hannah, I hope you're not serious or I'll most definitely have to decline your invitation. I'll go home and change."

"Nonsense, my dear child. You certainly wouldn't deny an old woman what few pleasures she has left in life. I've been looking forward to this ever since you called. Don't be cruel! I've always dreamed of having a daughter like you over whom I could dote and watch grow into a beautiful young woman. You've already grown into a beautiful young woman—now I want to enhance that beauty. Let an old lady indulge her whims while she is still able. Money was made to create beauty and pleasure. You would do me a great honor by letting me stun my friends and give some zip to the dull social whirl. I beg of you, Laura, don't deny me."

Laura was so moved by Hannah's impassioned plea, her eyes glistened with undeveloped tears. She rushed to the older woman's side and knelt down.

"Oh, Hannah, I couldn't refuse you anything," she said. She knew it wasn't right and she would feel guilty about it but her guilt was nothing compared to any happiness she might bring to the gracious though eccentric woman before her.

"Good! Shall we get started?" Hannah's smile was broad and triumphant as she stroked Laura's shining honey hair.

Bergdorf's department store hummed in discordant timbre and the cacophony of sounds had a rhythm and pace of its own. Visually it struck Laura as an abstract painting, sections of a vast canvas first dominating then receding yet still remaining part of the whole.

She strolled over to inspect a beautiful tan corduroy jacket displayed on a disdainful twig of a plastic model while Hannah conferred with a saleswoman, the latter scampering off in a flurry. She gingerly lifted the price tag then dropped it as if she had been stung by a wasp. Four hundred dollars for a jacket! Her entire winter wardrobe didn't cost that much. She was about to grab Hannah and flee the place when Hannah came striding toward her with an elegant, attractive woman beside her.

"Laura, this is Madame Piaget. She will be dressing you for the occasion."

Laura nodded a greeting, her eyes wide with awe and disbelief. At Madame Piaget's instructions, she meekly followed the graceful woman to a private, lush salon. At the mere clap of her hands, young women went scurrying about the place to satisfy Madame Piaget's demands.

When Laura saw the end results, she couldn't believe her eyes. Madame Piaget was a sorceress! She stared into the three-sided full-length mirror and felt like Alice in Wonderland gazing into that magical looking glass. Her transformation placed her in a world she had heard about but never thought she would be able to enter. The dark green emerald silk dress clung to her slim body as if it had been phosphorescently painted on. It hugged her waist, then cascaded down in billowy fullness to her ankles, where it dipped in diamond-like points, showing her calfs here and there. The matching silk-covered shoes added a touch of sophistication. The low-cut bodice, held by thin, rolled straps, left the smooth satiny skin of her shoulders and back temptingly visible. The front of the gown, cut straight and low, revealed a cleavage that promised well-rounded and full breasts.

Laura gasped as a matching cape with a silver satin lining was placed on her shoulders. The fact that Hannah was paying for all this didn't matter anymore, for she was sure it was all a dream and she would wake up any minute. From the corner of her eye she saw the appreciative gleam in Hannah's eyes and she knew everything was real—all too real.

"Madame Piaget, you have surpassed yourself," Hannah said and beamed.

"No, Miss Lawson. It is your young lady who has given the gown the grace it deserves."

Back at the brownstone, Laura luxuriated in a hot tub the maid had drawn for her. One of Hannah's preferred hairdressers was called in to do Laura's honey tresses when her bath and initial grooming had been completed. He dressed her hair in a becoming upsweep, leaving wisps of curly tendrils to frame her clear oval face.

Hannah smiled proudly and benevolently as they finished their dinner in the gracious dining room of the old brownstone.

"One more touch, Laura, my dear." Hannah rose from her seat majestically and went to the sideboard where a black velvet case lay waiting. "Stand up and turn around," she ordered, taking a strand of mixed emeralds and diamonds from their resting place. "Just the right touch. Not too gaudy but effective. You had better put the earrings on yourself."

Laura wanted to protest but was lost in a state of mute euphoria. She was Cinderella to a fairy godmother who had her completely under her spell.

The concert was a revelation to her, musically and spiritually. Itzhak Perlman had made the violin sing with an emotional exuberance that drained her. She stood and applauded with the same verve that affected the rest of the audience when the concert came to an end. She never saw the steely blue eyes riveted on her youthful body.

Out in the glittering vestibule, Laura was surrounded by a bevy of men whom Hannah was trying to introduce one by one with calm deliberation, much to the annoyance of the impatient gentlemen. The compliments she received made her head spin. Her eyes, moving from face to face, were suddenly drawn to a large figure towering above the crowd. She could never mistake that broad set of shoulders, the raven hair. It was the caretaker from Evans Mansion. A frown line creased her smooth white forehead. She couldn't comprehend his presence at the concert, much less in New York City. Her eyes slid to the dazzling creature on his arm. She could be a model, Laura thought, but her gown and glimmering jewels betrayed a longstanding wealth not usual for a model. A strong wave of jealousy gripped her. Red spots flared on her cheeks as she guiltily tried to stem the emotion. After all, she had no claim on him and, from past encounters, he certainly wished no part of her.

Her entire face turned scarlet when he turned and their eyes locked in recognition. Her heart bounced and the blood raced through her veins madly as he started to make his way through the crowd toward her, his eyes never leaving hers.

Relief flooded her as Hannah grabbed her elbow and steered her toward their waiting limousine, which quickly departed as soon as they were inside.

"Did you enjoy the concert, Laura?" asked Hannah.

"Very much," replied Laura, still breathless from the shock of seeing Bert Trebling.

"Well, I hope you enjoy the small cocktail party I've committed us to as much."

"Party?"

"As a patron of the performing arts, it is obligatory that I attend some of these functions occasionally. With you by my side, I can be assured it won't be boring. I'm rather looking forward to all the dandies trying to claim my mysterious and beautiful creature for their own."

"Hannah, you do exaggerate. There were many women at the concert who far outshined me in looks and probably in charm," argued Laura, thinking of the glamorous woman clutching Bert's arm and, at the same time, fighting back a twinge of envy.

"You have a certain quality of innocence, my dear, that men can't resist. It captivates and intrigues them. Besides, you'll meet a lot of people who might be willing to further the interests of your museum in Brooklyn. It'll be good for you," said Hannah, patting Laura's arm.

They were ushered into the spacious living room of the penthouse apartment belonging to an old friend of Hannah's, Cynthia Forrester. Hannah had told Laura of her old crony's considerable wealth and penchant for the arts—all the arts—and how she gloried in these extravagant soirees.

Laura expected to see a large, overdressed, domineering dowager and was surprised to find Cynthia Forrester a small birdlike woman, warm though twittery, elegant but simply dressed. No splashy jewelry.

"I'm so glad to meet you at last, my dear. Hannah has done nothing but talk about you since she's returned from her aerie in the islands. One would think she had found a long lost daughter. Come . . . let me introduce you to some of the people here," said Cynthia, smiling and drawing Laura's arm through hers.

It soon became a blur of faces and names. Laura couldn't remember which face went with which name and soon gave up trying. A glass of champagne had somehow found its way into her hand. She sipped at it as she became the silent member of a group discussing the acoustics of the various opera houses in Europe.

Almost spilling her drink, she turned as a warm hand caressed her bare shoulder.

"Kevin!" she cried in astonishment.

"You're so lovely, Laura," he murmured, drawing her away from the group to a fairly secluded corner. "I couldn't believe my eyes when I saw you walk in. I should have known old Hannah would take you under her wing immediately."

"I didn't know you were here. Were you at the concert?"

"No. I was having dinner with a potential client when he mentioned this party and how I should get to know Cynthia Forrester."

"Hannah tells me she is extremely rich."

"That and more. But right now, I'm more interested in you. I called several times but there was no answer."

"I've been working late trying to get things ready for the Harte exhibit. I'm looking forward to meeting the great man."

"I'm the only man I want you to look forward to meeting. How about tomorrow? It's Sunday. We could tour the city. See all the highlights of Manhattan. Take a ferry to nowhere. How about it, Laura?"

"I promised Hannah I'd attend church with her tomorrow morning, then go to the opera in the afternoon."

"Hannah will understand. She was young once," he pleaded and took her hand in his.

Laura shook her head. "She has done so much for me, I couldn't and wouldn't disappoint her. Don't you have some customers to wine and dine?"

"You're more important right now." He gazed at her warmly and smiled. Suddenly his gaze slid past her. "Oh, no!"

"What is it?"

"Here comes the dowager Forrester. Just when I thought I had you all to myself."

"Now . . . now . . . Mr. Courtney. I can't let you monopolize our lovely Miss Bickford. There are too many people who have been asking to meet her," admonished the petite woman waving a threatening finger at him.

"I find her too beautiful to share with anyone," said Kevin, giving Laura a wink.

"I'm afraid you can't have your way this time, dear boy. Besides, I think Jason Wentworth was looking for you. He has seen one of your designs and appears to be quite interested. I suggest you pin him down before something else takes his fancy. He has a very short attention span. He's the rather stout balding gentleman in the beige armchair near the fireplace."

With a small bow, Kevin planted a kiss on Laura's hand and headed for the beige chair.

"Charming young man, charming," cooed Cynthia. "Oh, well. Come along, Laura, I have someone who wants to meet you. Hannah tells me you are interested in the fine arts. This man is an artist, one of the finest in the country. This is the first time I've succeeded in getting him to attend one of my little gatherings. I daresay tomorrow it will be the talk of the art world," bubbled the small woman, glory shining in her eyes. "Oh . . . Mr. Harte," she called.

The tall, imposing form, impeccably dressed, turned and faced them. Laura felt as though someone had just hit her over the head with a club of iron. Her whole body pulsated as it pumped the blood from her face. The gasp that rose in her throat never reached her lips. She was staring into the cool blue eyes of Bert Trebling, the caretaker. Cynthia must have made a mistake, she thought, or the man was posing as the famous artist for some devious purpose of his own.

"Mr. Harte, may I present Laura Bickford." A wide smile fixed itself on Cynthia's face. "Laura, Nathaniel Harte."

"It is an honor to meet you, Miss Bickford." He took her trembling hand in his and brought it to his lips, scorching her skin. She glanced at Cynthia then back to the caretaker in total disbelief.

"Mr. Harte?" The incredulous tone in her voice was obvious. "You are—"

"I'm sure Mrs. Forrester wouldn't mind if I talked to you in private," he interrupted quickly and cast a melting smile at Cynthia Forrester. "Do you, Mrs. Forrester?"

"Of course not, Mr. Harte." She barely had the words out of her mouth when Harte swept Laura off to a quiet alcove just past the living room.

Laura's state of shock was quickly becoming one of anger. He had no right to drag her about especially when he had given her no explanation for his deceit and duplicity.

"What's this all about, Mr. Trebling? Why are you posing as Nathaniel Harte?"

"You have it backwards, Miss Bickford. I was Nathaniel G. Harte posing as Bert Trebling. The *G* stands for Gilbert. And Trebling is nothing more than Gilbert spelled backwards with an *N* added for easier pronunciation."

Her mind reeled under the impact of what he was saying. All the time she thought he was nothing more than the caretaker of Evans Mansion and . . . now . . . to learn he was Harte himself, the owner of the mansion spying on her and the work he himself had commissioned for her to undertake. What a fool she was! How could she ever have let herself think she was in love with him?

"Why did you lie to me?" she asked in a small tight voice. Her breathing grew more rapid as he stepped closer and she found herself backed into a wall.

"It seemed best at the time. I didn't want anyone to know of my presence in the islands."

"And you didn't think I knew how to keep a secret? Is that it?" she fumed.

He shrugged and placed his hands on her bare shoulders, causing her nerves to scatter around in discordant paths.

"You'll have to admit I didn't know anything about you. I had my studio in the attic and I didn't want a lot of people gawking about the place. And I was afraid if you knew who I was it might hamper the job you had to do. Besides, I rather enjoyed the anonymity. It gave me a certain amount of freedom." He smiled warmly at her with a tenderness in the depths of his blue eyes.

"How could you! Oh, you haven't changed a bit! It was contemptible of you to present yourself as an itinerant caretaker, letting me believe you were someone other than the famous Nathaniel Harte so you could spy on me. In view of such duplicity, Mr. Harte, I'll never again believe a word you say. I'd like to go now, so if you'll step aside . . ." She clenched her fists until her fingernails bit into the flesh of her palms while her heart was doing somersaults.

Harte's hands rose to the wall behind her, splayed on each side of her head as he leaned closer.

"You're not going anywhere until I've had a chance to make you understand."

"There's nothing to understand. Besides, any explanations coming from you would only consist of more lies and deceptions."

Laura saw the muscles in his neck tighten and there was a fury in his eyes she had never seen before. An alarming shiver gnawed at her spine as she moistened her dry lips with the tip of her tongue. His proximity and touch aroused a primal longing in her and her anger began to ebb.

"I'm sorry for being so rude," she whispered. "I was caught off guard."

"I probably deserved it, but coming from you it doesn't sound all that bad. You're all I've been—"

"There you are, Nat. I've been looking everywhere for you, darling." It was the beautiful woman Laura had seen him with at Lincoln Center. She possessively took his arm, which had fallen to his side at her intrusion. "What have you been up to, you naughty boy? You have this poor creature frightened half to death. Or is it your masculine charm that has her trembling so? Does she have a name?" The woman fluttered her long false eyelashes seductively at Nathaniel Harte.

"Deborah, this is Laura Bickford." He cast an inscrutable look at Laura. "Deborah DeWitt of *the* DeWitts."

"How do you . . ." Laura began extending her hand.

"Come along, Nat," ordered Deborah, ignoring Laura altogether. "There are *important* people here you should mingle with."

Harte threw Laura an icy stare and, much to her surprise, let himself be led away by the sultry Deborah DeWitt. She knew Bert, the caretaker, would have never let a woman lead him anywhere he didn't want to go.

She felt the need of a glass of champagne. Her nerves had been stretched taut by the knowledge Bert Trebling was really Nathaniel Harte and that he was here in the same room with her. She had almost drained her glass when Hannah appeared at her side.

"Why, child, you look as if you have seen a ghost. And your hand is shaking." Hannah paused reflectively. "I gather you've learned the so-called caretaker of Evans Mansion is in reality none other than Nathaniel Harte himself."

"Yes."

"It disturbs you?"

"Yes." Laura was close to tears.

"Wait here. I'll make our apologies to Cynthia and we'll leave."

"Hannah, there is no need for you to leave the party on account of me. Give me a minute and I'll have myself under control."

"We're leaving and that's that. Anyway, I find the evening becoming dull and the hour a bit late for my tastes. You'll be staying with me tonight. It's much too late for you to go all the way back to Brooklyn."

Silence reigned in the limousine on the way back to the brownstone. Hannah was lost in a world of her own and Laura's brain was numbed by champagne and the events of the evening.

In the morning, Laura's eyes fluttered open and the unfamiliar surroundings startled her. The last thing she remembered was being led to a room and flopping across a bed. Evidently someone had undressed her and put her to bed.

Before she could rise, a light tap sounded at the door and a maid in a crisp black and white uniform entered carrying a tray.

"Your breakfast, miss. I hope it meets with your approval. I'll draw your bath while you eat. Your clothes have been cleaned and pressed." She placed the tray on the bed, deftly flipping down the attached legs, then vanished.

Laura lifted the silver lid with one hand while taking the steaming cup of tea in the other. The scrambled eggs with thick slabs of ham on the side were complemented by peeled grapefruit and orange sections. Hot buttered toast stood at attention in its own silver holder. To her surprise, she devoured everything on the tray.

"Good morning, my dear," greeted Hannah as Laura entered the downstairs sitting parlor. "I trust you had a comfortable night."

"Yes, thanks to you. And also a lovely breakfast. You're spoiling me rotten, Hannah."

"Good. I enjoy spoiling you." She smiled mischievously. "Shall we go to church now?"

As they reached the sidewalk, where Hannah's limousine was waiting, a powerful hand grabbed Laura's wrist and held it firm.

"You're coming with me. You're going to hear me out whether you like it or not," the deep, resonant voice growled.

"Mr. Harte, being a fine artist is no excuse for rudeness," said Hannah, giving him one of her imperiously haughty looks.

"This is between me and Miss Bickford, Hannah, so stay out of it."

"Don't you dare talk to Hannah like that!" Laura's eyes blazed rebelliously. "You have nothing to say that would interest me. Now let go of my arm." She raised her chin proudly and willed her lower lip to stop quivering.

"I insist, Miss Bickford. My car is waiting," he said in a softer tone.

"Mr. Trebling . . . Mr. Harte . . . whoever you are . . ."

"Laura, my dear," interrupted Hannah, her eyes narrowing in contemplation. "Perhaps it would be for the best if you went with Mr. Harte and heard him out. There'll be other Sundays."

"No, Hannah. Why should we let him change our plans? Whatever Mr. Harte has to say can wait until after church," Laura declared, but her voice lacked conviction. She glanced from Hannah to Nathaniel Harte and loyalty became clouded with a peculiar longing. His touch was causing knots to form in her stomach.

"Go with him, Laura," ordered Hannah, climbing into the limousine, which quickly sped away.

Laura turned her bewildered and questioning eyes on Harte, who released her wrist but at the same time slipped his arm around her tiny waist and led her to the waiting silver Jaguar.

"Well, I'm waiting," she said as the sleek automobile made its way out of the city.

"In due time, Miss Bickford, in due time."

Laura sat back in the bucket seat with unhappy resignation. Nat's close presence disturbed her and aroused uncomfortable sensations. His strong, tanned hands gripped the wheel with assurance as they sped down the West Side Highway.

His masculinity dominated the small car. She turned her head to stare out the side window at the passing scenery, trying to focus her attention on each item as it went by as a ruse to keep her thoughts from the handsome and appealing man next to her. She couldn't weaken her defenses as she had done at the mansion. No. He couldn't and wouldn't win her good graces, not after his deception.

But her curiosity could no longer be contained as cement and steel gave way to trees, grass and wood frame dwellings.

"Where are you taking me?"

"To my home in Greenwich."

"Why? We could have talked in the city."

"I have my reasons."

"I presume they are honorable."

"I'm always honorable, Miss Bickford. Besides, I wouldn't dream of forcing my attentions on a young girl." He cast an unfathomable glance at her, then quickly shifted his stony gaze back to the highway in front of him.

"I'm not a little girl."

"I'm highly aware of that. But sometimes you act like one," he retorted, a vague smile forming at the corners of his lips.

An embarrassed heat filled Laura. Anger and chagrin mixed and raced through her brain when suddenly she came to the conclusion it wasn't love after all that she felt for this man but hatred—pure, unadulterated hatred.

"Look, Mr. Harte, I don't need or want your sarcastic insolence. It must be obvious to you by now that we have nothing in common except mutual animosity. Now please take me back to the city. There are many people at the museum capable of handling your exhibit. Under the circumstances I don't think I should have any part in it."

"I signed a contract with the museum and you are part and parcel of that contract."

"I take it then I'm nothing more than a part of a package deal?"

"You can take it any way you like. But I warn you, I'll cancel the exhibit if you back out now." Unexpectedly, he tossed her a broad smile displaying his white, even teeth.

When he smiled at her like that it dissolved any lofty aims of indifference she might have entertained. Every muscle in her body tensed. Her teeth gritted, her hands clenched and unclenched as her heart thumped erratically. She gave an inward sigh and prayed for the day to be over. Being with him was like having her heart chopped into a million pieces and scattered in the wind, and losing them on a breeze. The drive was beginning to seem interminable and, with reluctant resignation, she remained silent during the rest of the way.

CHAPTER 9

Laura expected to see some sort of rambling mansion and was taken by surprise to see a rather small house with an English Tudor facade as the Jaguar drove down the extensive graveled driveway.

With a swift catlike movement, Nat was around to her side of the car and had the door open. Taking her small hand in his strong fingers, he half pulled her along to the house. She had to make tiny running steps to keep up with his long, surefooted stride. His warm hand covering hers sent waves of desire through her. No matter what her opinion of him was, he was still capable of attracting her; sometimes beyond reason, she thought.

Once inside the house, he dropped her hand. His blue eyes were chilling as he gazed at her. They held a spellbinding glare that caused Laura to cringe imperceptibly. She realized it was foolish of her to have come with him, if not totally naïve.

"Will you please tell me what this is all about?" she asked calmly, trying to hide her trepidation.

His face became shrouded with indifference. "Is it always business before pleasure with you?"

"I find no pleasure in being here with you."

"I think our feelings are mutual. I'll dispense with the usual hospitable offer of coffee." There was a nuance in his voice that caused Laura to wonder at his meaning. "In fact, we'll dispense with any further pleasantries and get down to the business at hand."

"I would appreciate it. I want to return to the city as soon as possible," she said dryly.

"Follow me."

He led her through the tastefully decorated house where Queen Anne furniture played a dominant role. It didn't match the man, she thought. There was a quiet, gentle reserve about the place that did not fit the turbulent character of the man who owned it.

His studio was not the disarrayed jungle of paint and canvas she expected either. It was neat, orderly and gave the impression everything was very much under control.

"The twenty-two paintings I intend to lend the museum for the exhibition are over there." He waved in the direction of a group of neatly stacked paintings. "I think these are fairly representative of my work."

One by one, Laura surveyed his works as he placed them around the room or on empty easels. She hadn't realized the full extent of his skill and talent. These paintings had an impact that was unsurpassed, at least for her. The sensitivity of his paintings belied the coarse, rough man she had come to know.

"Is it too much to assume you will give proper thought to the lighting and framing of these?" he asked, his voice mocking and rude.

But Laura didn't hear him. She was immersed in a study of the works of art before her, captivated by them. They had the plaintiveness of a Wyeth, the vibrancy of a Turner, the subtlety of a Manet and the pathos of a Daumier.

Nat leaned against the wall watching every phase of Laura's changing expressions as her eyes leaped from one painting to the next. A broad smile curled on his wide lips. Some time had passed before he broke the silence.

"Well . . . what do you think?"

Bewildered by the bombardment of her senses, visual and emotional, she hesitated then said, "Magnificent . . . just magnificent."

She wanted to add, How could someone with your disposition paint pictures that hold an acute awareness of life and color with such insight and warmth? Her gaze met his as the question ran through her mind and when he returned her gaze with a steady intensity in his steely blue eyes, life fluids seemed to drain from her body. She felt weak, hot, cold, vibrant, all at the same time. He stared down at her, his look intensifying until she could no longer stand the raw seduction in his eyes. She turned her attention back to the paintings.

"I'll do my very best to present them to the best advantage," she said in a shaky voice.

"That's all I ask." He started toward her but stopped and went to the door instead, as if his mind had changed course in midstream and decided on another direction. "I'll take you back to the city now."

The cold, impersonal tone of his voice snapped Laura back to the reality of her practical, business relationship with this man. What had she expected? A romantic interlude in Connecticut? Did she really think he would sweep her into his arms and kiss her until she was no longer herself? Or had she hoped . . . desired . . . dreamed he would? Her whole body convulsed as the moments on the island flooded her heart and mind. To be in the same room with him again —so near and yet so far—made her weak with longing to feel his arms around her, his mouth devouring hers. Maybe if she had been a little less caustic with him . . . well, it was too late now for what-might-have-beens.

The ride back to the city was shattering. He could have been cruel and sarcastic and she would have felt more at ease. But he said nothing. He brought the car to a jarring halt in front of her apartment. It never entered her head to ask him how he knew where she lived. Her mind was occupied elsewhere. He reached over and opened the car door for her. The rich masculine scent of him assailed her nostrils with a heady delight, then the smell of burning rubber erased the fragrance as he roared down the street without even saying good-bye, his face set in stony indifference.

Laura brushed her hair with a vigor that bordered on rage. She no longer wondered why she had these feelings of anger. She knew. She was hopelessly in love with a man who thought of her as a female possessed and obsessed by her career; the kind of woman he wanted nothing to do with. He never saw her as the warm tender woman she wanted to be whenever she was with him. She shrugged carelessly. Maybe that's all she was deep down, totally oriented and committed to her career. She certainly never gave him any reason to think otherwise. Her hand paused in midair, brush still in hand, as she visualized those precious moments at Evans Mansion when he held her in his arms, when he kissed her so deeply. At least she would have those memories.

It was Hannah who rescued Laura from a bleak social life, taking her to concerts and operas. It had become a ritual. Hannah's limousine would pick her up in Brooklyn every other Saturday morning, returning her to the apartment late Sunday night. Hannah's brownstone had become a home away from home for her.

As the days went by, Laura found herself doing something she had never done before, scanning the gossip columns in the papers. Every so often, there was an item regarding the artist Nathaniel Harte, and the beautious creature constantly by his side, Deborah DeWitt.

She kept trying to tell herself it was none of her business what he did or whom he saw. He was a free agent and with the exception of a few brief moments when isolation and proximity had thrown them together, had never given her any reason to believe she meant anything to him other than a woman who was there when he felt the need of one. But she did find it difficult to understand why this man, who had made his aversion to women a clear and palpable fact, was all of a sudden in the steady company of one particular woman. She refused to acknowledge the possibility he might be in love with Deborah DeWitt.

"You've been far away this weekend, Laura," said Hannah as they finished Sunday dinner. "The Harte exhibit is next week, isn't it? Is that why you are so preoccupied?"

"I'm sorry, Hannah. I didn't mean to be rude or such rotten company. Yes, the exhibit is next week and I do hope everything goes well."

Hannah stared at her hard. "Maybe I'm wrong but an old woman's intuition tells me there is something more than the exhibit on your mind. Harte himself, perhaps?"

"I didn't think it was so apparent." Laura smiled faintly. She knew it was impossible to keep anything from Hannah. The woman had a sixth sense about everything, especially where Laura was concerned.

"I knew it!" Hannah beamed triumphantly. "I've been selfish in abducting you every weekend when you could have been with him. Why didn't you speak up, girl? Didn't you think I'd understand? No one is more enthralled by romance than I. You should have known that by now, my dear."

Laura gave a small half-laugh. "I'm afraid Mr. Harte isn't enthralled by romance. At least, not with me."

"But . . . that dreamy expression on your face that creeps up every once in a while . . . oh, yes . . . don't think I haven't noticed it, young lady. You show all the unmistakable signs of a woman in love and I do believe for the first time. What is it, child? A lover's quarrel?"

"I'd be happy if it were that. No . . . he isn't even aware of me as a woman."

"Then make him, child. Love is a precious and elusive gift. Once it comes, don't let it slip through your fingers like grains of sand. Close your hand and hold it fast."

"Oh, Hannah, if only it were so simple," she sighed. "He's in love with someone else and couldn't care less if I were on this planet or not."

"Don't underestimate yourself. You are a very beautiful young woman. Why, you saw for yourself how the men swarmed all over themselves to be near you every time you appeared at some event. And more importantly, you're a sweet person. I can't think of anyone who outshines you," said Hannah emphatically.

"No? Well, I can."

"Who?" Hannah's eyebrows arched.

"Deborah DeWitt."

"Deborah DeWitt? That plastic-coated piece of marble? Her fuel emanates from dry ice and emits no warmth at all. Harte is all man. He wants more from a woman than she could ever hope to give him." Hannah's lips pursed in thought while an amused twinkle invaded her eyes. "So it's Harte, is it?"

Laura nodded and took a sip of the tea in front of her. It was cold.

"When did it happen? At the mansion?"

Again she nodded, not knowing what to say.

"Well, my dear, he looks like he's worth getting. If I were you, I'd go after him, DeWitt or no DeWitt."

"More than once he's told me to my face he has no use for my sort. No, Hannah. I will not make a fool of myself by chasing a man who I know can't tolerate me and despises the sight of me."

"Well, I know I wouldn't give up without a jolly good fight. Is there anything I can do to help?"

"I appreciate your concern, Hannah, but I'm sure I'll get over him and survive. Sometimes I wonder what I see in him. He's sarcastic, insulting, egotistical and arrogantly aloof. I'm surprised he even allows himself to be seen with the DeWitt woman. She must have qualities I know nothing about. She certainly isn't the type I ever thought the caretaker of Evans Mansion would fall for."

"Men are perverse creatures at best, my dear." Hannah sighed deeply. Seeing the subject was painful for Laura, she changed it. "Next weekend we'll do the town. Maybe we could fly up to Boston for the weekend. Would you like that, my dear?"

"I'm sorry, Hannah, but Saturday is the private showing of the Harte paintings and Sunday is the official opening of the show. Being in charge of everything, it is my duty to be there. Besides, I'm anxious to hear all the comments firsthand. You'll be coming Saturday night, won't you? I made sure your name was on the list for exclusive invitations."

"I wouldn't miss it for the world. Is Harte going to be there?"

"He'd better be, or Mr. Donaldson will have a heart attack on the spot." Laura gave a strained laugh.

"Good girl. Laugh. It is the panacea for all the ills of the world."

Over the next several days Laura was in a whirl. The paintings had arrived at the museum and she had to decide on the proper frames, lighting and hanging of them. She also had to make sure the small catalogs and brochures were printed and delivered on time.

For the private showing, there were the cocktails and hors d'oeuvres to attend to, which seemed to Laura an insurmountable problem until Cynthia Forrester came to her rescue. Being an old hand at special showings of any kind, Cynthia secured the services of caterers who specialized in large cocktail parties. And, to Mr. Donaldson's delight, Cynthia insisted on footing the bill.

When Saturday finally came, it was a nightmare. Frames were missing, lights failed to function properly, paintings were hanging askew, Mr. Donaldson was running about nervously, shouting orders then countermanding them.

It was shortly before six in the evening when order began to set in. The frames were found, the wiring corrected and the paintings hung square on the walls. Mr. Donaldson had left an hour early in a state of battered confusion and despair, much to Laura's relief. Things were accomplished with greater ease without him.

She had little more than an hour to get home, bathe, eat, dress and be back at the museum before the show opened at eight-thirty.

A mixture of disappointment and surprise washed over her face when she saw Kevin Courtney's strong frame leaning against the door to her apartment.

"Kevin!"

"I expected a warmer greeting than that," he said, his grin disarming as ever.

"You couldn't have caught me at a worse time, Kevin." She fumbled in her purse for the key, which seemed to have a mind of its own whenever she was in a hurry. "You'll have to excuse me. The Harte exhibit opens tonight and I have a million things to do before I have to get back there." She found the key at last and swung open the door. Kevin hastily followed her in.

"Here I brave the perils of Brooklyn to reach you and now you tell me you have to work. I'm crushed," he teased.

"You should have called first, Kevin."

"I know. Look, as long as I'm here is there anything I can do for you?"

"You could make me a sandwich and get some coffee going while I take a bath."

"No sooner said than done, my lady."

She rushed into the bathroom and started a tub liberally sprinkled with bath salts, whose aroma quickly filled the steamy room. She didn't have time to take the leisurely bath she had planned but soaked long enough to purge the ache from her weary body, sending new vigor through her. With a towel turbaned around her head and covered with a thick terry cloth robe, she emerged to find Kevin had made her an omelet, toast and freshly brewed coffee.

"You're a godsend, Kevin," she said, sitting down at the table and greedily attacking the food.

"And you're a goddess. You should never wear makeup. You are far more beautiful without it." The admiration in his eyes was genuine and Laura blushed. "How long is this shindig of yours supposed to last?"

"It's hard to say. Perhaps a couple of hours, perhaps past midnight. I really don't know."

"I was going to suggest I stay here and wait for you. We could have a late supper or some pizza."

"I have a better idea. Why don't you come with me?"

"I'm not the arty type."

"Big money tonight, Kevin. Some of the wealthiest people in New York will be there."

"Now you've aroused my interest."

"And Hannah will be there to introduce you and so will Cynthia Forrester," Laura urged, then drained her coffee cup.

"What are we waiting for? Go get dressed."

In the bedroom, she blow-dried her hair, then brushed the satiny tresses until the color shimmered like rare jewels. She slipped into a cerulean blue silk sheath whose simplicity and color emphasized the warm curves of her body and the opalescence of her skin. Kevin's earlier compliment danced in her head and she applied a minimum of eye makeup with no other cosmetics. The result pleased her. Her lips and cheeks had a natural rosy flush of their own she hadn't noticed before.

"Am I presentable?" she asked, twirling around for him to see her from every angle.

"We'd better go," he said hoarsely, "before my impulses get the better of me."

Never had Laura seen so many people gathered in the special exhibition rooms. Her eyes unconsciously scanned the crowd to find the tall, dark figure of Nathaniel Harte. Her heart raced in anticipation but he was nowhere to be seen.

"Shall we look for Hannah, Kevin?" she asked nervously as they mingled with the crowd.

"Well, if it isn't the dashing Mr. Courtney and Hannah's young protégée. How opportune!" gushed Cynthia Forrester, taking hold of Kevin's arm and balancing a glass of champagne in her other hand. "You don't mind if I steal him away from you, do you? I know several people here who would be delighted with your talents, Mr. Courtney."

She led him away through a maze of people, chatting away as Kevin threw Laura a resigned look over his shoulder. A uniformed waiter, who was unobtrusively wending his way through the throng, held his tray for Laura's inspection. She took a glass of champagne and continued her search for Hannah. Her attention was drawn to a painting she hadn't seen before. She was positive she knew every painting on display. How could this particular one have escaped her scrutiny? It was a fascinating canvas and she was sure she would have remembered it. But the frame was nothing like the ones she had ordered. The painting must have been hung after she left, she concluded. It might even have been brought to the museum after she left. It didn't matter, for the painting was an absolute treasure. It was the portrait of an older woman sitting on a red velvet couch. There was a compelling aura about it and the haunting eyes mesmerized Laura. It was as if she had known the woman or had seen her before somewhere.

While she tried to prod her memory, she felt a large, strong hand encircle the nape of her neck. She pulled her head forward and glanced around but the hand remained firm as she looked into the vibrant blue eyes of Nathaniel Harte. He was close behind her and she could feel the warmth of his body radiating into hers.

"Do you like that painting?" His deep voice sent shivers along her spine. She took a long sip of the champagne, hoping it would give her the courage and enough wit to answer with the sophistication of a Deborah DeWitt. A weak, muffled "yes" was all she could manage. Who could be worldly and clever when their knees were shaking?

"My mother," he announced and turned his eyes from her to look at the painting.

"She is a beautiful woman."

"Was. She passed away a number of years ago." His eyes swung back to Laura and roamed over her face and slender form. "She had a warmth and simplicity about her that is lacking in most of the women today. She believed in the innate goodness of people. A romantic to the core." He smiled, softening the sharp bone structure of his face.

"I haven't seen this picture before. I was wondering how it escaped me."

"At the last minute I decided to show it. I hadn't intended to originally. Luckily some of the men were still here and I had them hang it. You had just left."

His hand on her bare back and his smile were making her deliriously self-conscious. She would never understand his fluctuating moods. One minute he was treating her like a leper, the next like an old friend. She went to take another sip of the champagne, only to find her glass empty.

"Come along. We'll get you another glass. But don't drink too much of the stuff or you'll regret it tomorrow. Champagne gives one a nasty hangover."

His warm, broad hand slid down her back to encircle her waist. For one insane moment, she had the feeling he was going to sweep her up in his arms and whirl her around the room in a soundless waltz.

He deftly lifted a glass from a passing tray and handed it to her, his other hand never leaving her waist.

Congratulations were given by serious-minded men and fluttering women, the latter obviously under the spell of his rugged good looks. His arm remained possessively around her regardless of who tried to draw him away. Even though she was at a loss to understand his behavior, especially when he had so silently dismissed her at their last meeting, she was in heaven until Deborah DeWitt made a belated entrance to the exhibition.

Nat's arm tightened spasmodically around Laura's waist as the regal Deborah glided toward them, people moving aside to let her pass. Laura smothered a small giggle as a vision of Moses parting the Red Sea flashed across her mind. She even thought Deborah looked as stern and foreboding as Moses himself, if not more so.

Pearly white teeth were framed by bright red lips as Deborah smiled at them icily.

"Darling!" she cooed at Nat and kissed the air by his cheek. "Do forgive my boorish tardiness but my stupid chauffeur got lost. Brooklyn! The absolute hub of provincialism! I'll have some champagne, my dear, then you can show me your pictures. I don't believe I've seen these before," she declared while slipping her hand through Nat's free arm and ignoring Laura's presence.

She was sure Deborah had noticed Nat's arm around her waist. Although her actions and words never gave her away, her eyes did. The malice in them was overwhelming. As Laura felt his grip slacken, she whispered, "Excuse me" and slipped from his grasp, quickly losing herself in the crowd. It was with a sinking heart she realized Nat was only using her to stir the jealousy Deborah was swift to display.

Tears were starting to shimmer in her eyes as she defiantly put her empty glass on a tray and took another full one. Starting to feel a little giddy as her sips became larger, she went in search of Kevin. To her relief and delight, she literally ran into Hannah instead.

"My goodness, child. One would think the devil himself was after you." Hannah squinted her eyes and peered at Laura. "Why I do believe you've had a bit too much of that bubbly grape juice."

"It's very relaxing, Hannah, very," she muttered, slurring her words.

"Well, I shouldn't think you would need any champagne to lift your spirits. From what I've been hearing, the exhibition is a smashing success. Everyone thinks the presentation is impressive to say the least. You've done an excellent job, Laura."

A huge smile skittered across Laura's lips. She had forgotten all about whether or not people would like what she had done when Nat had come on the scene.

"That's marvelous . . . marvelous!"

"Give me that glass, young lady. You've had enough of that. Come along. There's a coffee urn in the entry. I think you could use some about now."

"But I was looking for Kevin," Laura protested feebly.

"Kevin can wait," declared Hannah as she took the young woman's arm and led her to the waiting coffee urn.

After two cups of the steaming liquid, Laura's eyes started to focus more clearly.

"Do you realize, young lady, you were on the verge of being drunk?" Hannah admonished.

"I'll have to admit I was feeling a little strange. I probably should have eaten a more substantial supper. In the excitement today, I skipped lunch and only had coffee and a piece of toast for breakfast."

"Good Lord, child. What are you trying to do to yourself? With the energy you expend, you should have three square meals a day. Maybe I should make you move in with me."

"Aside from my mother and father, you are the sweetest person I know." She kissed Hannah lightly on the cheek.

Despite her effort to staunch it, Hannah flushed. "Would you like me to have my chauffeur drive you home? Your presence isn't really necessary now."

"I came with Kevin. I shouldn't sneak off and leave him."

"Don't worry about Kevin. He left about thirty minutes ago with a distinguished-looking gentleman. A prospective client, I presume. He's a real go-getter, that boy."

"I'm surprised he didn't let me know he was leaving."

"He looked for you but ran into me first. I told him to go ahead. I'd let you know as soon as I saw you."

"In a way I'm glad he's left. I'm not up to spending a late night."

"I'll have my car come around for you."

"No . . . don't bother, Hannah. I'm going to the office. There are a few things I should take care of. Besides, I want to be here after everyone's left to make sure everything is in order."

"As you wish. But don't fall asleep and get locked in the museum for the night."

"I'll leave the door open. The acoustics there are peculiar. I can hear everything in the gallery as if I were there myself. When it starts to quiet down, I'll come and check."

"I'll call you later in the week, my dear."

The sound of Laura's heels against the marble floor of the corridor echoed with a strange resonance. As promised, she left the door open and turned on the small desk lamp, which illuminated sheaves of papers strewn on the otherwise neat desk top. She sat in the chair and began to sift through them, making notes in the margins here and there. She could still hear the muted voices emanating from the distant galleries.

Some time had passed when she felt a wave of uneasiness wash over her and a sense of foreboding began to gnaw at her concentration. Someone was watching her. She looked up quickly and instantly recognized the herculean form casually leaning against the door frame. With the hall light behind him, his shadowy countenance appeared satanic and ominous.

"Is that all you think of . . . work?" he asked when he saw he had been discovered. He effortlessly pushed his body upright and came toward her.

Her throat constricted as her heart pounded. She found herself speechless as his sensuous mouth twisted in an odd smile. She recalled his hand softly tracing down along her neck to her back, stirring smoldering flames deep within her. The recollection sent particles of heat bouncing over the surface of her skin.

"Am I so terrifying you can't even speak? Or have you decided to give me the silent treatment?"

"No . . . you startled me," she finally managed to say.

"Well?"

"Well, what?"

"Why are you here working when you should be out in the galleries singing my praises?"

"Aren't there enough people out there to do you homage?"

"Don't be infuriating, Miss Bickford, constantly answering a question with a question."

"The exhibit, I understand, is a smashing success. I've done my job, so I didn't think my presence was required any longer," she replied, mouthing the same excuse Hannah had made for her.

"I saw Hannah pouring all that coffee into you," he said, grinning. "A bit tipsy were you? Don't say I didn't warn you."

"I don't think my state of being is any concern of yours. I'm quite capable of taking care of myself."

"I'm sure you are. All career women seem to have that brittle core of undeniable independence," he teased, an amused sparkle in his eyes. "But I didn't come here to argue with you, Miss Bickford. I came to congratulate you on the exhibit. You've done an admirable job."

"I don't know, Mr. Harte." She began shaking her head. "You have all the characteristics of a chameleon. Do all artists have such mercurial temperaments?" She flushed at the unforeseen compliment.

"Only when they are faced with perplexing and difficult young ladies," he said in a low, captivating manner as he came around the desk and inched closer to her.

"Don't you think it best to rejoin your admirers in the gallery?" she asked, her head spinning as she swung it back to the desk and fumbled with the papers there.

"They can wait."

"I wouldn't make them wait too long if I were you, or Miss De-Witt will have to come and fetch you and probably give you a good scolding for not doing as you are told." The minute she said it she wished she hadn't. It was a dumb thing to say, especially when he had gone out of his way to be nice to her. He had a way of rattling her thought processes and making her say things she really didn't mean. The look of raw outrage on his face was enough to terrorize the calmest heart.

His two hands came down on her bare shoulders and lifted her out of the chair. His eyes softened as they linked with hers. He gently pulled the combs that held her topknot in place and tossed them on the desk without taking his eyes from hers. Her blond hair cascaded with a burnished gloss around her pallid face.

Before she could catch her breath, as if to punish her, his mouth came down on hers with a searing impact, forcing her lips to part. His kiss softened and became more probing with a gentle persuasion. She felt herself being swept along in an eddy of mounting desire. As if he had been kissing her like that all her life, her pale arms crept around his neck, into his hair, as she returned the kiss. She could feel his hands leave her shoulders and wind around her slim body in a crushing embrace. She could feel every taut, sinewy muscle of his body through the thin silk dress. It was a heady pleasure arousing her senses to an unbelievable height. It was like being on the edge of a precipice where one more step would bring total oblivion, utter destruction. Try as she might to fight it, she knew she was at the point of no return as her heart pulsed in time to his. It was useless to deny she loved him with all her heart and she always would, regardless of his erratic behavior. If only she had the courage to tell him, but she knew her pride would never let her do so.

"Well!" Deborah's shrill exclamation brought Laura back to reality with a crash and she extricated herself from Nathaniel Harte's embrace as he, too, turned, completely startled.

"I hope I'm not intruding on your moment of fun, Nathaniel, but most everyone of any importance is getting ready to leave. We've been asked to join Cynthia's entourage and have a midnight snack at her place. I'm sure there'll be more toys there for you to play with if you so desire. . . ." Deborah's voice dripped with a chilling venom.

"That's enough, Deborah!" Nat snapped harshly as he angrily stalked toward her.

Embarrassed and confused by the emotions plaguing her, Laura started to giggle nervously without really knowing why. Nat threw her a quizzical look that had a twinge of pain in it, but it quickly turned to an impersonal mask of superiority laced with a touch of discomfort.

"Let's get out of here and go to Cynthia's." He grabbed Deborah's arm and half dragged her out of the office, but not before Deborah cast a haughty look of triumph at Laura.

That night Laura lay in bed and bittersweet tears trickled from her eyes onto the pillow. Every time she closed her eyes, she saw the look of indifference Nathaniel Harte gave her as he left the small office. Why did she have to laugh? He might have ignored the DeWitt woman and stayed with her. His kiss had been sincere and loving—that she was sure of. All of it addled her brain until she was no longer sure what she thought. Maybe Deborah was right. He was only having a bit of fun with her, teasing her, using her to arouse Deborah DeWitt's jealousy. Well, she thought, I certainly gave him his money's worth by dissolving in his arms at a mere touch. Oh, why did he have to come back into her life? Why did he show moments of great and endearing tenderness only to end them with a peculiar apathy?

She dismissed the thought of asking Hannah to take her to Bermuda with her. That would be running away. Laura knew she must face him and deal with her emotions or she wouldn't be able to live with herself. She had survived the trauma of unrequited love with Peter and she'd survive this. But somehow, in her heart, she knew this time it was different.

CHAPTER 10

The accolades for her work on the exhibit boosted Laura's sagging spirits. Once the paintings were safely returned to Nathaniel Harte, when the exhibition was over, she would have no further contact with him. There would be no reason for it. The thought of never seeing him again stirred an aching melancholy in her but it was tempered by a sense of relief.

She had told Hannah about the incident in the office the night of the private showing and Hannah did her best to rationalize the event in Harte's favor, but it was to no avail. Laura was adamant about avoiding him. She made Hannah promise not to take her anyplace where Harte might make an appearance, and reluctantly Hannah promised.

The offer of dinner and the theater from Kevin Courtney came unexpectedly. She had been inclined to refuse but Hannah thought the outing would do her good and help to get her mind off Nathaniel Harte, as Kevin had a natural ability for lightheartedness. In deference to Hannah, Laura accepted Kevin's invitation.

"Sorry I had to run out on you during the Harte show but business called and I wasn't about to pass up a good thing," Kevin apologized as the waiter poured their wine. After ordering their food, he continued, "Hannah assured me she would take good care of you and see that you got home safely."

"Don't give it another thought, Kevin. How did you make out with your 'distinguished-looking gentleman,' as Hannah phrased it?" she inquired, wanting to draw the conversation away from the subject of the private showing. She wanted to blot it from her mind.

"A commission."

"Marvelous!"

"I never realized how lucrative the Manhattan market could be. Cynthia said Fairfield County in Connecticut and Long Island had even more possibilities. It seems the upper middle class has taken a fancy to boating and as the number increases the cabin cruisers take on a sameness that the very rich want to avoid. So . . . they are seeking personalized designs that will set their boats apart from the run of the mill. Not everyone wants a big yacht but they do want something highly original. The market is wide open and I'm ready to embrace all of it."

"Then it looks like you might be staying in the city for a while." Laura sipped the wine slowly, remembering her foolish imbibing of the champagne.

"Quite frankly, I'm thinking of selling the boatyard in Alexandria Bay and concentrating on design only."

"You wouldn't, Kevin. I thought you loved that boatyard of yours."

"I guess I do, in a sentimental way. It wasn't until I had the yard that the big, big commissions started coming my way. I suppose I should keep it as a talisman if nothing else. It certainly pays its own way. But this itinerant life has some compensations. For example, I got to see you again and much sooner than I had expected. And more importantly, I have been swept away into a world I knew existed but never dreamed I could be part of. The horizons are inexhaustible. It would be nice if you would share it with me."

"How many commissions have you received while here in the city?" She avoided his eyes. The conversation was taking on a serious tone that she was in no mood to deal with.

"You're ignoring me, Laura. Every time I try to nail you down you shy away like a frightened rabbit. Is there something about me you find distasteful?"

"Oh, I'm sorry, Kevin. I really didn't think you'd take my evasions personally. It's me . . . I'm not . . . well . . . you're a very nice man and I really do enjoy your company but . . ."

"But you're not in love with me, is that it?"

Laura nodded. She couldn't bring herself to say the words. The silence that hovered about the table as they ate dinner was unbearable for her. She wanted to ease the tension but couldn't think of anything clever to say.

"Well, I never did go for that love bit," Kevin finally said, looking relieved. "But we could still have a lot of fun together, Laura."

"You sound much too busy to waste time having fun."

"I'll have to admit New York City has been a veritable grab bag of orders. I put my hand in and it comes back with a large commission. Before you know it, I'll be in their financial league," he gloated, raising his wine glass in a mock salute.

"I hope so, Kevin. If anyone has earned it, you have."

"Hey, we'd better get a move on if we don't want the curtain to go up without us," he exclaimed, glancing at his watch.

The play was a comedy and soon both Kevin and Laura had forgotten about their brush with the more solemn side of life. They laughed in the cab on their way to Brooklyn every time one of them mentioned a phrase or act from the play.

"Really, Kevin, we could have taken the subway. A taxi all the way from Manhattan is an unnecessary extravagance," she said as they walked up the cement steps of her apartment house.

"I'm moving into the big league, remember?"

"Are you sure you won't come up for a cup of coffee?"

"Quite. I'm heading out to the Island tomorrow and need an early start. Besides, cabs are hard to find around here at this time of night."

"Thank you for everything, Kevin. I had a wonderful time and I do wish you the best of luck tomorrow." Laura stood on tiptoe and, resting her hands lightly on his arms, gave him a light kiss on the cheek.

Suddenly Kevin's arms were around her and his mouth on hers, strong and demanding, belying his seemingly gentle nature. It made her extremely uncomfortable, for the only man that could make her come alive was Nathaniel Harte and that was a love that would never be.

"No bells?" Kevin asked as he released her.

She shook her head, then murmured, "Sorry."

"Well . . . win a few, lose a few," he laughed. "But it's always a pleasure to take out a beautiful and charming woman. See you in a week or so." He bent over and gave her a brotherly kiss on the cheek before bounding down the steps to the waiting taxi. Laura had the feeling Kevin would survive the rejection quite well and she wouldn't have been the least bit surprised if he had someone else waiting in the wings. Another Peter, she thought with a sigh, only Kevin was open and honest about his intentions.

Laura proudly took Hannah to Vermont to meet her parents for the Thanksgiving holidays. She spent the four days showing Hannah the wonders of the Vermont countryside, where they spent most of their time walking and talking. Hannah was charmed by the simplicity and genuine affection Laura's parents showed her and was at a loss for words when Mrs. Bickford gave her a framed piece of crewelwork she had done.

On one of their walks before leaving Vermont, Laura took Hannah down to one of her father's favorite fishing streams. They walked along it as Laura searched for the exact spot her father claimed to be magical.

"It's obvious your mother and father are proud of you and your achievements, Laura, but I noticed a wistful look in your mother's eyes every now and then. I have the impression she would have chosen another path in life for you," Hannah stated intuitively.

"You've always been a keen observer, Hannah. Yes, my mother's fondest dream was to see me safely married. Although I never knew why she thought marriage was any guarantee of safety."

"I think it is instinctive for people our age and generation to believe a woman's only shelter in life is marriage. Possibly in our time it was. But in this day and age there are other alternatives open to women that weren't available forty or more years ago. On the other hand, your mother perhaps wants you to love and be loved, with the kind of love that is peculiar to a man and a woman."

"I know what it is to love a man, Hannah."

"Ah, yes, Nathaniel Harte. And if he returned that love, what would you do?"

"Probably die of joy."

"I'm serious, my dear. Do you think you could tolerate his capricious moods? His peculiar whims?"

"Without a second thought. I have a feeling it's all a facade anyway, for there have been moments when he proved he could be the tenderest of lovers." Laura's eyes glazed wistfully as they studied the ground. She shoved her hands in her pockets and smiled despondently.

They walked along in silence, the dead leaves of autumn crunching crisply beneath their feet. An occasional blue jay would hawk a solitary note in the chill November air as he flew among the barren branches of gray spidery trees.

"I can see why you come here as often as you can, child. It is beautiful and peaceful, much like my little island."

"There it is," said Laura, pointing to a spot in the fast-flowing stream. "I don't know if father catches as many fish as he says he does, but when he comes back from one of his fishing jaunts there is a whole new spirit about him."

"The water is so clear," remarked Hannah as she leaned over the mossy bank. "I don't see any fish though."

"Don't feel bad. I've never seen any fish in this stream either," Laura laughed.

"I could do with a good hot cup of your mother's tea about now. Shall we start back?"

Laura nodded. As the house appeared on the small knoll ahead of them, Hannah took Laura's arm.

"Don't sell Nathaniel Harte short, my dear. He's a man like the rest of them. Nothing is hopeless."

"In this case, I think it is," Laura sighed. "It seems every time I think he feels something for me, he switches to absolute indifference."

"It might be his method of defense, of remaining noncommittal. He's a man of deep emotions. His paintings evince that. It could be he's afraid to love knowing it would be a lifetime involvement for him."

"And it could be he just doesn't like me. No, Hannah, I will never throw myself at him, or any man, for that matter."

"I'm not suggesting you throw yourself at him. I only think you should keep an open mind and don't reject him outright when he becomes irrational. Good Lord, girl, you're lovely enough to make any man irrational. Give him and yourself a chance. Promise?"

"All right, I promise but I won't let him make a fool of me. Anyway, this whole conversation is pointless, for I shall probably never see the man again now that the exhibition is over."

"You thought you'd never see the caretaker of Evans Mansion again either."

A few days after their return to the city, it was with a deep sense of loss that Laura accompanied Hannah to the airport, where the latter was about to commence her annual journey to Bermuda.

"I wish you'd change your mind and come with me, my dear. Bermuda is refreshing this time of year. A far cry from the cold, damp, slushy snow of the city."

"You shouldn't tempt me so, Hannah. You know I have to work for a living."

"Not really, my dear. You could be my companion and travel around the world with me."

"It's sweet of you to offer, Hannah. But I do enjoy my work and my friends—all of which will keep my mind occupied. I'm afraid the kind of life I'd lead as your companion would leave too much time to think. Right now, I want to keep as busy as possible."

"The young men I could introduce you to would keep you quite busy, I assure you."

"You know how I feel. I've got to sort it all out in my mind and come to grips with it. In time, I suppose I'll learn to live with it."

"Well, do as you must, child. The offer will always be open to you."

A mechanical voice boomed through the lounge announcing arrivals and departures.

"I'd better get along or the plane will leave without me. Take care, my dear, and keep me informed." Hannah kissed her on the cheek and the latter responded in kind. "I'll let you know where you can reach me. I expect a torrent of letters from you. Be good to yourself and I'll see you in the spring."

Tears welled in Laura's eyes as she watched the huge plane soar up into the sky until it was lost to view. She sighed and went back to the parking lot where Hannah's limousine waited. As the chauffeur took her to Brooklyn, she felt as though she had lost a loved one. She hadn't realized how deeply attached she had become to the older woman. She would miss their weekends together. Cheer up, she told herself, spring was only a few months away and she had her friends until Hannah came back. Meanwhile, she hoped for a new assignment at the museum. Something she could really sink her teeth into.

The entire museum was in an uproar when Laura arrived at work the next day. The Harte exhibit was over and had been a huge success, so she couldn't understand the reason for all the undue excitement.

"Oh, Laura, am I glad you're here," exclaimed a flustered Mr. Donaldson, mopping his balding brow with a well-crumpled handkerchief.

"What's happened?"

"Mr. Harte called. He claims one of his paintings is missing."

"Are you sure it wasn't one of those that had been sold?"

"It was the only one that wasn't for sale. The portrait of his mother. We've been looking for it everywhere but can't find a trace of it anywhere."

"I sent a list of the sold paintings to Mr. Harte and then packed everything that hadn't been sold myself. I distinctly remember having the portrait of his mother crated with the rest of the paintings. Who delivered them?"

"Why, Mr. Harte picked them up himself. He was particularly upset when you weren't here. He felt it was your duty to give him a personal accounting."

"Did you explain to him I went with a friend to the airport?"

"Yes, but it only seemed to agitate him further. Right now our main concern is to find that painting. I always thought you were a reasonably level-headed young woman, Laura. I never thought you were the careless kind. What have you done with that picture?" pleaded Mr. Donaldson, his eyes bulging in fright as he nervously twisted his handkerchief.

"I can't imagine what could have happened to it."

"You'll have to do better than that. You have to find it. Try to remember what you did with it. Maybe you didn't put it in the crate with the rest of them but laid it aside somewhere, then forgot about it. Do something! I'm at my wit's end."

"I'll do my best, Mr. Donaldson." She was truly puzzled and searched her mind for some clue as to its possible whereabouts. She was certain she had crated it along with the others. She was never careless where works of art were concerned.

What could have happened to it? Was Nathaniel Harte playing some sort of trick to discredit her? Was he trying to portray her as a reckless, irresponsible person not trustworthy enough to be assigned important tasks? Did he dislike her that much?

She began a methodical search for the missing painting while the others returned to their normal duties. Every so often Mr. Donaldson would frantically question her success or lack of it.

After several hours of hunting the premises and at an utter loss, she hesitantly sought out Mr. Donaldson in his office.

"Excuse me, sir."

"You found it, Laura?" asked Mr. Donaldson, looking up hopefully from the pile of papers on his desk.

"No, I'm sorry to say. But I would like to ask you a few questions if that's all right with you."

"Well? Ask."

"Did anyone help Mr. Harte carry the paintings out to his car?"

"No. In fact, he insisted on doing it himself, come to think of it."

"Was his car parked directly in front of the museum or off to the side door?"

"I don't think I even saw his car. If I remember correctly, he went downstairs and out through the back door."

"Thank you." Laura turned and swiftly left Mr. Donaldson's office. She took the route she thought Nathaniel Harte might have taken when he left the museum. She looked in every alcove, in every corridor, any place where one could conceivably hide a painting. But it was no use. Impulsively, she had truly believed he had hidden it and was out to ruin her reputation as assistant curator and impugn her integrity. But she hadn't found a thing and could only conclude he hadn't hidden it. She had let her judgment of the man be colored by her own imagination. He certainly wouldn't take the chance that the painting might be damaged just to make her look negligent. No artist would.

She started down the long empty corridor where the storage rooms stood sentinel on each side of the highly waxed linoleum floor. For some intangible reason she stopped before the music room, where old instruments were kept for special exhibits. An idea popped into her head for an exhibition of these instruments. It had been some time since they were tuned and polished for show. And what a coup it would be if she could convince some prominent musicians to perform on them on specified occasions. Her mind began to whirl with the possibilities. She opened the door spontaneously and, confronted with the darkness, switched on the light.

She gasped audibly to see the portrait of Nathaniel Harte's mother resting boldy on an old harpsichord.

"That devil!" she cried aloud. Her hands balled into fists and her lips pursed in frustration. He was playing games with her after all. Relief to have discovered it tempered her initial anger.

She carefully lifted the painting from its musical perch and proceeded upstairs to Mr. Donaldson's office.

"You found it!" Pure joy flooded Mr. Donaldson's rotund face as he jumped to his feet.

"Yes. It was—"

"Never mind that now. The important thing is that you found the painting. I must call Mr. Harte immediately and tell him the good news."

Laura stood impatiently tapping her foot while Mr. Donaldson dialed the phone. Her mouth tightened in a hard line and she wished she were the one dialing Nathaniel Harte. While Mr. Donaldson's voice droned on in the background, she fantasized about the biting and cleverly barbed words she would have said to the man. So intense was her concentration on composing some stinging rhetoric, she didn't hear Mr. Donaldson addressing her.

"Laura! Miss Bickford!" His pinched voice finally broke through her wall of self-indulgent reverie.

"I'm sorry, Mr. Donaldson. What were you saying?"

"I said Mr. Harte wants you to deliver the painting to his home in Connecticut first thing in the morning. He said you know where the place is."

"Yes, I do. But I'll have it insured and send it up there by special delivery."

"No . . . no . . . that will never do. Mr. Harte was quite explicit. He said it was your fault the painting was misplaced and he felt it was your duty to return it in person."

"Oh, he does, does he? Well, he can take special delivery instead. I don't have the time to go chasing all over Connecticut to return a painting he deliberately—"

"Why, Miss Bickford, I'm surprised at you! I've never known you to be so outspoken."

"Maybe it's about time I was!"

"Please calm yourself. I'm perfectly willing to give you the day off to deliver the painting. After all, Mr. Harte is a distinguished artist and I wish to accommodate him in any way I can. If you wish to remain employed here you'll deliver the painting, in person, first thing tomorrow morning and that's all there is to it. Meanwhile, I'll put the painting in here where I know it will be safe and where I can find it."

Laura stomped out of the office angrier than when she came in. Now this rogue was in a position to threaten her job. Oh, how she wished she had never heard of Evans Mansion. It should be a rule that all caretakers be men who are very old or very married.

The next morning she arose exceptionally early as she wanted to take a steaming shower and have a substantial breakfast before heading into the nearby suburbs of Connecticut. She also wanted to plan a scathing tirade for Mr. Harte's benefit. She wasn't going to be caught tongue-tied this time.

After the shower, breakfast and several mental notes, she started to search her closet for something suitable to wear. It would be colder in Connecticut than it was in the city. She chose a cocoa brown suit and the amber-colored cashmere sweater Hannah had bought her because it matched her eyes. With her dark brown cape and boots, the outfit would be striking, she thought.

She entered Mr. Donaldson's office still composing and refining the little speech she intended for Nathaniel Harte. She would tell him off once and for all. She was even beginning to look forward to the visit with a certain amount of relish.

"Is the painting ready, Mr. Donaldson?" Her eyes sparkled with anticipation.

"Ah . . . I'm afraid there has been a change in plans, Laura. Miss DeWitt has graciously consented to return the painting to Mr. Harte. She said she spoke with him last night and he agreed it would be easier than having you make a special trip, seeing as she is going there anyway." He waved his hand in the direction of Deborah De-Witt.

Laura spun on her heels to see Deborah calmly sitting in a chair off to the side. In her absorption in planning revenge, she hadn't noticed the woman when she came in. She made no move to greet Deborah; she could only stare at her, her mouth slightly agape.

"There is no reason for you to go out of your way, Miss—?"

"Bickford," Laura snapped.

"Yes. Miss Bickford. As I was saying, there is no reason for you to go. I'm going there myself today and I'd be delighted to take the painting and ensure its safety."

The cool crispness of Deborah's voice rankled Laura. There

seemed to be an insinuation she wasn't capable of delivering the painting intact. And it also seemed strange that Harte would insist she deliver it personally, then suddenly change his mind. It wasn't like the man. Once he made up his mind, nothing in the world would change it. She had the distinct impression that the whole idea was a ruse thought up solely by Deborah DeWitt to keep her away from Nathaniel Harte, as there was some uncertainty in the other woman's probing eyes.

"I'm sorry, Miss DeWitt. My instructions were quite clear. I am to deliver the painting personally. I would be remiss in my duty if I didn't carry them out to the letter. It was my error and I intend to correct it. Of course, if you wish, we can call Mr. Harte and tell him why I'm not following his direct order."

"Aren't you being a bit childish, Miss Bickford? Or is it that you don't believe me?" Deborah's smile was venomous.

"I've learned never to take anything for granted, especially hear-say." Laura returned Deborah's smile but her eyes betrayed a deter-mination to see the confrontation through.

"Mr. Harte is a very busy man. I think you'll find your intrusion on his privacy would be most unwelcome."

"Now, ladies," interjected Mr. Donaldson, reaching in his pocket for his handkerchief.

"Didn't you inform me yesterday that my job would be on the line if I didn't deliver the painting personally, Mr. Donaldson?" fumed Laura.

"Why, yes . . . yes, I did. But perhaps under the circumstances . . . Miss DeWitt . . ." he shrugged absently.

"Well, I'm not about to lose my job because someone might have misinterpreted Mr. Harte's wishes. I understand he was quite em-phatic yesterday, isn't that so, Mr. Donaldson?"

"Well . . . yes."

"Have you heard anything to the contrary?" Laura asked.

"No . . . I haven't talked to Mr. Harte since yesterday," said Mr. Donaldson, looking from one woman to the other cautiously.

"Then I think we should leave things as they are," Laura stated firmly.

"Well . . ." Mr. Donaldson's voice trailed off as his eyes lowered to study his desk top.

"I think you are making a great mistake, Miss Bickford. But what you decide is no concern of mine. I was just trying to be helpful." Deborah rose from the chair with catlike ease. "Thank you for your time, Mr. Donaldson. I'll make sure Mr. Harte doesn't take offense at the museum for the actions of one individual." She paused at the door and, after a moment's hesitation, turned to Laura, the smile returning to her face. "As long as I'm going to Nat's, I'll be happy to give you a lift," she said as her eyes narrowed to study the young woman.

"No, thank you. I have my own car."

"Oh, that's right. How negligent of me. You'll have no way of getting back. After all, I'll be staying there for some time." She haughtily swept out of the room but not before giving Laura a smug, cutting glance.

Making sure the painting was carefully placed in the back seat of her car, Laura started out for Connecticut wishing the DeWitt woman hadn't had such a head start on her. She had wanted to catch Harte unaware of her arrival. She knew Deborah would tell him about their little discussion in Donaldson's office. She was also sure Deborah would meet her at the door and snatch the painting from her and slam the door in her face before she even caught a glimpse of Nathaniel Harte. Her well-rehearsed diatribe would never be heard.

To her surprise, a portly woman opened the door when Laura rang the bell to Nathaniel Harte's home. She found herself looking into a pair of merry eyes set in a large oval face whose chubbiness was stressed by the severely pulled back gray hair.

"Hello. I'm Laura Bickford. I've brought Mr. Harte's missing painting with me. Is he at home?" she asked, returning the infectious smile.

"Oh, yes, miss. He's been expecting you. He said to have you wait in the living room and he'll be with you shortly."

Laura clutched the top of the painting as her knees started to shake at the thought of seeing Harte again. His presence, his towering physique, the strength of his arms, the masculine scent that pervaded a room when he was there—all made her breath come in rapid gulps. She knew she had to get control of herself if she was to say everything she had planned.

Looking about the room, she examined every object with careful scrutiny . . . anything to take her mind off the imminent meeting with Harte. Her gaze fastened on the large fireplace and she remembered grasping the poker to ward off the man she had come to love so deeply. A wistful smile formed on her lips and she could almost hear the Strauss waltz. Her eyes lifted to the faded square spot over the mantel and it was the same size as the painting she was steadying with her hand. *That is why I hadn't seen it when he showed me the canvases in his studio. It had been hanging over the fireplace,* she thought, knowing she had never been in this room.

If he thought so much of the painting, why did he jeopardize its safety by leaving it in the music room? It might have gone unnoticed there for some time. She would have thought the painting meant more to him than a means of discrediting her abilities. She shook her head slowly; she would never understand the man. He was like a chameleon, slipping in and out of moods as easily as one would a robe.

"I see you found the place, Miss Bickford."

Laura watched Deborah DeWitt glide into the room as if she had done it a thousand times before. She eased herself into a chair and sipped the clear liquid in the cocktail glass she held in her hand. Her red silk tunic dress was extremely becoming, making her look like a glossy model from *Vogue* magazine. Everything about Deborah was perfect from her long slim legs to her sharply pointed, bright red fingernails. Laura began to feel a trifle dowdy in her dull brown outfit, which she had originally thought was quite smart.

"Why do you persist in standing there like a frightened schoolgirl clutching onto her last hope? You've delivered the painting safe and sound, so why don't you lean it against the chair over there and leave? I'll tell Nat you were here with the portrait like a dutiful little girl." Her voice was cool and smooth, almost slippery to Laura's ears.

"As I told you, when I'm assigned a job, I carry it out to the letter. I was told to deliver it to Mr. Harte and deliver it to him I shall." Not even Deborah DeWitt was going to rob her of the pleasure of speaking her mind to Nathaniel Harte. Besides, she didn't like the high-handed way Deborah was trying to get rid of her.

"How noble! Are you always so conscientious? Or are you trying to worm your way into Nat's personal life? If you want some advice, I don't think he would appreciate that," she cooed with a sneering smile frozen on her bright red lips.

"The last thing in the world I want is to become a part of Mr. Harte's personal life," Laura fibbed, knowing how Deborah would grind to dust her true feeling for Harte. She tried to staunch her growing anger at the woman's blatant insolence. She could see that Deborah was attempting to bait her and Laura was determined not to play her game.

"Really now! You certainly have a peculiar way of going about it. You know very well I could have brought the painting with me but you insisted on bringing it yourself. That's a strange way of avoiding what you least desire, isn't it?" Deborah took another sip from her glass, her calculating eyes remaining fixed on Laura as she peered over the rim.

"There is a personal message I have to give Mr. Harte that you couldn't convey."

"I'll bet there is, little Miss Innocence."

"And what do you mean by that?"

"It seems to me you were a little too careless in misplacing a valuable painting. That is, if it was misplaced."

"What are you suggesting, Miss DeWitt? That I deliberately held it back in order to see Mr. Harte?" Though her voice was calm, her flashing eyes betrayed her irritation.

"I won't say it didn't cross my mind."

"I didn't think you had one for anything to cross."

"My . . . you do have claws after all."

"Only for the purposes of defense. I'm not the predatory type."

"Most women are the predatory type. Some admit it, some don't. You are one of those who won't admit it, not even to yourself."

"And in which category do you fall, Miss DeWitt?"

"I'm one of those rare exceptions. I don't have to be predatory. You see, I have all the prey I want or need. They flock to me whether I beckon or not. But I doubt if you even know what I'm talking about."

"You mean like vultures to carrion? I understand you are an extremely wealthy woman, Miss DeWitt." The minute the words were out of her mouth, Laura wished she hadn't said them. She was stooping to Deborah's level with backhanded, catty insults. But the woman was beginning to rile her and Hannah had told her to fight for what she wanted.

Deborah swirled the liquid around in her glass and stared at its curling motion. "You're becoming quite tiresome, Miss Bickford. In fact, you're quite boring. You've accomplished your little mission, so why don't you leave?"

"I'll wait for Mr. Harte, thank you." Holding on to the picture, Laura sat down on the sofa opposite Deborah, causing the latter to quickly rise.

"Listen, Miss Muffet. You can get off your tuffet and get out of here. You're not welcome but you don't seem to have the brains to see that." Deborah's face was crimson with rage.

"Do you always order other people about in someone else's house?" asked Laura calmly. She was beginning to enjoy this repartee. Hannah would be proud of her.

"Get out! Before I physically drag you out of here." The words were hissed, low and menacing, as Deborah trembled with raw fury.

"Do you always get the shakes when you drink? They have help for that you know, Miss DeWitt."

"You little . . ." Deborah threw her glass into the fireplace. "Get out of here before I . . ."

"Before you what, Deborah?"

CHAPTER 11

Startled, both women turned at the sound of the deep masculine voice.

"I repeat, Deborah, before you what?" Nathaniel Harte stood in the doorway of the living room. Laura's heart bounced in her throat at the sight of him.

"Oh, Nat, I'm so glad you're here," purred Deborah, rushing to his side and linking her arm through his. "This wretched creature has gone out of her way to be insulting no matter how hard I tried to be pleasant to her."

"Poor dear!" He patted her hand. "I know she is a very trying young woman."

His eyes bored into Laura, making her wish she had left when Deborah first suggested it.

"She's brought the painting, Nat, now have her leave. I find her behavior upsetting and her manner annoying."

"I had the feeling she'd upset you so I took the liberty of having your chauffeur bring your car around. Mrs. Peale has your coat."

"What? Me? Leave?" Deborah stared at him in total disbelief. "But Nat, I was under the impression we were to spend the day together, then leave for Cynthia's party tonight."

"My dear Deborah, you have the uncanny knack for creating false assumptions then making yourself believe them. I wasn't aware I even invited you here today."

"When I telephoned you last night, you seemed to indicate you would enjoy my company." Deborah pouted.

"Did I now? You certainly have an active imagination, Deborah. You're keeping your chauffeur waiting."

"That's what he gets paid for," she replied bitterly. "What about her?" She waved her hand in Laura's direction without so much as a glance.

"I have some unfinished business with Miss Bickford."

"Well then, I'll wait in the other room. I'm sure whatever business you have with her won't take long and we can continue with our plans as scheduled," she said defiantly.

"Evidently you didn't hear what I said, Deborah. I want you to leave. It's as simple as that." He looked down at her and even Deborah knew by his stern visage he wouldn't stand for any further disobedience from her.

She released his arm and headed for the door but turned as her hand touched the knob.

"You won't forget about Cynthia's party tonight, will you, Nat?" There was a sharp edge to her voice.

"No. I won't," he answered with a trace of exasperation.

"I'll see you tonight then, darling." She gave a slight toss of her head as she left the room, like a person who has won the battle after all.

Laura rose to her feet as Nathaniel's steely blue eyes focused on her.

"There was no need to send Miss DeWitt away. I only came to deliver the painting personally as you requested." Her need to verbally abuse him had vanished in the heated conflict with Deborah. Her anger was spent.

"Just a minute." He caught her by the arm as she started past him. "I want you to unwrap the painting to make sure it hasn't been damaged in any way."

Laura didn't want any more arguments. Her bout with the DeWitt woman had been enough for one day. She had used up all her clever retorts so she meekly unwrapped the painting.

"Are you satisfied?" she asked, displaying the unharmed painting.

"Careless of you not to include it with the others, Miss Bickford." A bemused smile hovered at the corners of his mouth.

"Me? Careless of me? How dare you! You know very well you yourself hid the painting in the music room downstairs."

"Now why would I do a thing like that?" His eyes sparkled at her gleefully.

"To discredit me at the museum."

"Discredit you?"

Laura was surprised to see he was truly shaken by her accusation. But this man had fooled her before and she wasn't going to let herself be taken in by the hurt and bewildered look on his handsome face.

"Don't try to deny it, Mr. Harte. I may not be one of your favorite people but I never thought you'd stoop so low as to jeopardize my job. Or have you decided to start a private crusade ensuring the destruction of all career women?"

"My dear Miss Bickford, you have me all wrong. I'm not out to ruin your career or anyone else's for that matter."

"I'm not your dear Miss Bickford. And I can't think of any other reason for you to pull such a stunt."

"Can't you? Did you ever think it might have been a simple ruse to bring you here?"

"What for? To be insulted and humiliated by your Miss Deborah DeWitt?"

"She is not *my* Deborah DeWitt!" he countered.

"According to Miss DeWitt, you are most definitely *her* Nathaniel Harte."

Nat's eyes narrowed with amusement as he looked down at her. "Do I detect a note of jealousy, Miss Bickford?"

"Me? Jealous? Jealous of what, may I ask?" She did everything possible to keep her emotions bottled up inside her. She had to display the same inscrutable expression he was so expert at.

"The glamorous, alluring, wealthy Miss DeWitt."

"Hardly. I'm afraid I would never really feel comfortable in her world. Hannah Lawson has given me a rather large taste of it and I know it's not for me."

"What kind of world is for you, Miss Bickford? The world of the constant scramble to the top? The dog eat dog struggle for survival in the world of competition? Do you really prefer that kind of existence to one of caviar and champagne?"

"You amaze me, Mr. Harte. Your paintings display all the various gradations of color yet you seem to think only in terms of black and white. Is that how you really see life?"

"I see you haven't lost the ability to answer a question with a question." He walked over to the portrait of his mother and gazed down at it. "Life for me is never black and white, Miss Bickford, but, with the exception of my mother, it seems the women I have known had a tendency to view life in those terms. I had assumed you were no different."

"What was it you accused Miss DeWitt of? Never make false assumptions?"

"Touché!"

"My career, as you put it, is not the all-consuming passion of my life."

"What is?"

"To be happy, I should say. I think that's everyone's main goal in life, when you come right down to it, don't you?"

"Happiness is a very elusive quarry, Miss Bickford. Do you think you can capture it? Or is it already in your grasp?"

Laura smiled softly. "I've known moments of happiness," she replied, thinking of the ballroom in Evans Mansion and the man who whirled her around the floor so magnificently.

"Then you are fortunate indeed, Miss Bickford. It has always been just beyond my reach."

"Surely your fame as an artist has brought you some measure of happiness. I know it would me if I possessed such a talent."

"Ah, fame and fortune . . . everyone's key to happiness. If you reach the pinnacle of your career . . . became the absolute authority in your field . . . bringing the world to your feet, would you be happy?"

"I never really thought about it all that much. It would bring a kind of happiness, I suppose."

"But not true happiness, I expect. But enough of this speculative philosophy. It was never my strong point." He picked up the portrait and studied it.

"You told Miss DeWitt you had some business with me?"

"Always business with you, isn't it, Miss Bickford. It's a shame that behind that pretty face of yours is a one-track mind."

Laura could see this discussion was going to end like all the others —a contest of opposing views. She breathed a sigh of remorse as he went to replace the painting over the mantel. With his height, it was a simple task. While he was preoccupied positioning the picture, she thought it best to leave before she let herself be drawn into a futile argument with him. She couldn't bear the thought of their last meeting ending in a petty quarrel. She was about to place her hand on the door knob when he spoke.

"Are you leaving, Miss Bickford?"

The man must have eyes in the back of his head, she thought. "Yes, I am. I have to get back to the city."

"Why? Oh, yes. I suppose your Mr. Courtney is waiting with open arms for your arrival."

With an impatient sigh and a somewhat melancholy look glazing her eyes, Laura turned to find he had completed his chore and was regarding her intently. "Look, Mr. Harte, I'll call a truce if you will. Our business with each other is over and there is no reason for us to see each other again. Couldn't we try to end on a friendly note?"

He smiled at her and there was a glowing warmth in his brilliant blue eyes; her heart melted on the spot. She wanted to run and throw her arms around him in wild abandon. How she remained rooted to the spot was beyond her.

"For once, I agree with you, Miss Bickford. I invited you to my home and I should at least try and act the gracious host. As a small measure to atone for my boorish behavior, I wish you to stay and have dinner with me."

"Aren't you forgetting your engagement this evening? Cynthia's party?"

"I'm not forgetting it. I never had any intention of going in the first place."

"What will Miss DeWitt say?"

"I don't give a damn what Miss DeWitt says or does."

"I thought . . ."

"You thought what?"

"Well, that . . . you and her were . . ." Laura stammered. She couldn't put her thoughts into words after his comment about the DeWitt woman.

"Deborah and me?" His laughter was deep and resonant. It was several seconds before he regained control over his mirth. "Deborah was handy and always available. Perhaps she thought we were an item, or are, but believe me, there was no way that woman was going to get her claws into me."

"I should have known from past experience no woman would ever get that close to you, you wouldn't take one seriously."

"I thought we were going to call a truce."

"I didn't mean it as an affront. It was only an observation."

"Then you'll stay for dinner?"

"Do you really want me to?"

"There you go again. When will you learn to give a straight answer? You should know by now if I didn't want you to stay I wouldn't have asked you."

"Yes, Mr. Harte. I'd be delighted to be your dinner guest."

"Good. Now you're learning to answer a question properly."

He took her hand, raised it to his lips and kissed it. "Let me take your cape." His hands were on her shoulders before she knew it. "Would you flee the house if I told you I have an ulterior motive for wanting you here?"

"It depends on what your motive is," she replied, her eyes wide with apprehension and her blood setting fire to her veins.

"I want to do a portrait of you."

"Of me? Why?" His words stunned her.

"Being an artist, I don't need a reason. I either feel a painting or I don't. There is a quality about you I want to put on canvas. Do you find that so hard to believe?"

"Considering our past encounters, yes, I find it hard to believe."

"Personalities have nothing to do with an artist's need to create, Miss Bickford."

"I'm afraid you've forgotten the obstacles to such an undertaking, Mr. Harte. I'm a working girl, remember? And the opportunities to sit for you would be few and far between."

"I'm sure we could work something out. It really won't take that many sittings. I'll only need two or three to get the general outlines in and the mood of the painting."

"Well . . ."

"I won't take no for an answer." He took her hand and drew it through his arm. "Come."

He led her up the stairs to the attic studio where the ceiling was studded with huge glass panels flooding the vast room with an opalescent light. A heavily constructed easel dominated the room. It already bore its burden of a large canvas as if it had been a foregone conclusion she would sit for him.

He seated her in a red velvet chair and positioned her to his liking. The very touch of his hands on her arms caused her to flush with excitement.

She watched him slip into an old, paint-smudged linen coat that bore a resemblance to that of a fledgling doctor. He went about preparing his paints with the precision that comes from years of experience. He seemed totally unaware of her presence, for he neither spoke nor motioned to her.

At first the time seemed to fly by, but as the minutes turned to hours, her muscles became taut, her body ached from the rigid pose. She had pangs of hunger and the more she thought about it, the more her desire for some food increased. If only she could have something to quench her thirst.

Out of desperation she asked, "Would it be too much trouble if I had a glass of water?" At this point she didn't care if she disrupted his mood or not.

"Of course not," replied Nat, and he glanced at his watch. "For God's sake! Why didn't you say something sooner. It's after two o'clock. You must be famished. I'll have Mrs. Peale fix us a light lunch."

"You were so intent I didn't want to disturb you," she said, rising from the chair.

She started to step forward and, without warning, fell to the floor. Her right leg had crumpled beneath her like a wet paper bag. From the long hours of posing, her leg had fallen asleep and become insensate.

Nat rushed over and collected her in his brawny arms. He lifted her up and she had no recourse but to lean heavily against him as her leg slowly tingled back to life.

"What happened? Are you ill?" he asked, his strong arms holding her tight to his body.

"I think my leg fell asleep, that's all."

"It's my fault. I should have known better than to let you sit in one position for so long." His broad hand pressed her head to his massive chest so firmly she could hear the beat of his heart. Unshed tears of joy played in the corners of her eyes when she felt him kiss the top of her head.

"It's all right now. I think I can stand on it," she said haltingly.

His arms loosened their grip but he did not let go of her entirely as her feet touched the wooden floor. He ran the back of his hand down the side of her face gently, then with one lean finger tilted her chin back so she was looking directly at him.

"Miss Bickford . . ." He paused for what seemed an eternity, then nervously cleared his throat. "Shall we see about some lunch? Do you think you can manage the stairs?"

Laura nodded meekly. She didn't trust her voice.

The potato salad and cold ham were like a feast for a king, Laura thought. Her hunger, so great by now, would have devoured cold hot dogs with ravenous zest.

"Well, Miss Bickford, what is your next project or major effort for the museum?" His face was impassive as his voice resumed its usual impersonal tone.

"Things are usually fairly quiet around the museum during the holidays. I don't expect any spectacular assignments or project until after Christmas and the New Year," replied Laura, trying to match his air of indifference.

"Does that disappoint you?"

"No. I look forward to the peace and solitude of Vermont."

"Vermont?"

"Yes. I sometimes spend the holidays with my parents, at least a portion of them."

"Aren't you afraid you'll miss out on some big scheme at the museum while you're away?"

"Not in the least. Whether you believe it or not, there are things in life that take precedence over my job. Surely you don't paint seven days a week. For example, you took time off to play caretaker at Evans Mansion, or should I call it the Harte Mansion now?"

"No. For historical reasons it will remain the Evans Mansion. But you are mistaken to think I walked around and played at janitorial duties all the time. I had a studio set up in the attic. That is why those floors were shut off. I never thought I'd have to deal with a curious young lady. And if you had seen my work, I'm sure you would have guessed my identity and that would have ruined my seclusion."

"Will you be going back next summer?" she asked, wishing she could turn back the clock and relive those moments spinning around the great ballroom in the arms of Nathaniel Harte.

"I doubt it."

"Why not? It's such a beautiful spot."

"It wouldn't be the same now."

"Because you've opened it to the public?"

"Something like that. Anyway, there are new places to explore."

A strained silence hung in the air as Laura averted her eyes from his intense gaze. She absently stirred her coffee, desperately trying to think of something to say to ease the growing tension.

"Tell me, Miss Bickford, you say you have priorities other than your job. Why haven't you ever married? Or isn't that one of them? A lovely girl like you must have been asked at one time or another."

"I've never been in love before."

"And you are now, I take it." His face hardened into a mask.

"Yes." She couldn't lie about it. But he would never know that the man sitting across the table from her at that minute was the one she loved more deeply with each passing minute.

"Would you mind sitting for a few more hours before the light goes?" he asked stiffly. "Perhaps I can get the mood I'm seeking in one more sitting; then I won't have to inconvenience you by asking you to come back."

"No. I'm quite rested now." The chill in his voice made her heart sink. There had been brief moments in the day when he seemed more than friendly toward her. She had even dared to hope she saw a semblance of affection in his eyes now and then. She sighed audibly as she rose from the table.

"If you find it too much of a strain, Miss Bickford, we can dispense with the sitting altogether. I know how anxious you must be to get back to the city. After all, I'm sure Kevin Courtney is far more entertaining than I. I wouldn't want people to think Nathaniel Harte went about ruining other people's happiness." There was an irritation in his voice that verged on resentment.

She stared at him in wonder, not knowing what she had done or said to vex him. "I thought I was invited to dinner. I fail to see what Kevin Courtney has to do with it."

His implacable blue eyes looked into her soft, innocent amber eyes. "I would like you to dine with me this evening. I only thought . . ." Again the nervous clearing of the throat. "Promise me you'll tell me the moment you begin to feel tired or cramped."

"I promise."

She had never seen a highly acclaimed professional artist at work, only students and teachers at the school and perhaps an occasional apprentice in the museum copying an old master. Nat's concentration and dexterity fascinated her. When he looked at her his face was immobile. Only when he worked on the painting itself did his countenance take on diverse expressions.

She watched his handsome face as shadows began to fall across the large studio and wondered if he was going to try to paint in the dark. She felt pangs of regret that the day was almost over as he stood back from the easel and began to clean his brushes.

"Well, I think that will do for now. As the light started to fade it lent the mood I was trying to capture. I'm quite pleased. It was an excellent sitting. I'm sure you could do with a bracing cocktail about now. I know I certainly could."

"I'd prefer some cold white wine if you have it."

"Anything you wish. White wine it is."

He left her downstairs in the living room while he readied their drinks. It was relaxing to sit in the large overstuffed armchair in front of the fire so expertly started by Mrs. Peale. She leaned her head back and closed her eyes. Her neck ached from having to hold her head erect for so long a period of time. It was a relief to let her entire body go limp. It startled her to find Nat staring at her when she opened her eyes.

"Your wine, Miss Bickford," he said, extending a delicately etched glass toward her.

"Thank you."

"I think Mrs. Peale has surpassed herself tonight. The aroma in the kitchen is tantalizing. I do hope you're hungry."

"It's odd. I've done nothing but sit all day and yet I'm ravenous."

"Good. She would be disappointed if you didn't eat anything."

"Were you pleased with the show?" Laura asked for want of anything better to say.

"Yes. Very much so. To tell the truth, it went beyond my expectations. I didn't think I'd sell that many paintings."

They turned toward the door when Mrs. Peale announced dinner was ready. Laura rose, taking her glass with her, and went into the formal dining room, Nat close behind her.

Their conversation over dinner was banal and forced. Laura had the distinct feeling he was sorry he had asked her to stay and wanted the evening over with as soon as possible. He spoke to her politely but she knew his mind was occupied elsewhere. He toyed with his food while she devoured everything put before her, relishing every

morsel. She felt those cool blue eyes observing her every move and
wondered if he thought she was a glutton.

"Mrs. Peale is an excellent cook. Everything is so delicious," she
stated defensively.

"I'm glad to see you are enjoying it."

"You're fortunate to have Mrs. Peale to do your cooking."

"She only comes in for special occasions. I usually fend for myself. You should be thankful I didn't subject you to one of my culinary forays."

Before Laura could reply, Mrs. Peale came in with the coffee.

"Will there be anything else, Mr. Harte?" she asked as she started
to clear the table of the used dishes.

"I don't believe so, Mrs. Peale."

"Dinner was superb, Mrs. Peale. You are an excellent cook,"
Laura said with genuine admiration.

"Why, thank you, miss." Then to Nathaniel Harte, "Will you be
wanting me tomorrow, Mr. Harte?"

"No. I don't think so."

"Then I'll say my good night now and clear up the kitchen before
I leave. I'll be here on Thursday as usual, Mr. Harte."

"Fine. Good night, Mrs. Peale."

There was a strange, grim expression on Nat's face at the departure of Mrs. Peale. Laura sipped her scalding coffee, keenly aware
of the growing and arduous silence. The sound of the back door closing echoed like a sonic boom throughout the house.

Laura raised her head and forced herself to meet his steady gaze.
Suddenly she was deeply aware of the perilous, mesmerizing effect he
was having on her. With Mrs. Peale gone, they were the only two
people in the house. What am I so afraid of? she asked herself,
knowing deep down she knew the answer. It wasn't Nathaniel Harte
she was afraid of but herself. The weakness that consumed her whenever he looked at her. The way her blood drained to her toes whenever he touched her. The madness that fired her flesh and obliterated
her reason when he kissed her. A shudder scampered through her
and though it half burned her throat she gulped down the coffee in
huge swallows. She had to get out of there before she literally threw
herself into his arms.

"It was a lovely dinner and I thank you but I really must be going.
It's a long drive back to the city."

"I'll take you back."

"No . . . no. I wouldn't dream of having you go out of your way.
I've done it many times before, coming back from Vermont," Laura
said quickly. She wanted to get away from him before she could no

longer resist his magnetic power and acted foolishly. She would rather die than have him think she was some puerile romantic.

Nat looked at her sharply, the corners of his mouth set in a hard line, his jaw thrust forward.

"I understand. The city really doesn't come to life until well after dark. I'll get your cape, Miss Bickford. I am not so boorish as to keep a young lady from enjoying her pleasures." He stomped off, leaving her standing with her mouth agape.

She tried over and over again to keep Hannah's words in her mind. She was determined not to leave on a note of discord and false impressions, but he precluded any friendly gestures by saying, "I think you know where the door is," as he thrust the dark brown cape toward her.

She fumbled with the frog fasteners before they finally slipped into place. Murmuring a thank you, she rushed out of the house before he could see the tears starting to well up in her eyes. She picked up speed as her feet hit the graveled path to where her car was parked. Haste bred carelessness and she soon was flat on the ground with a twisted ankle.

She sat up stiffly, glad Nathaniel Harte wasn't around to see her awkward position, then rubbed her sore ankle, but rubbing through the boot wasn't much use. It was only a second or two before her peripheral vision spied the two feet planted beside her. Apprehensively she looked up at the giant of a man staring down at her.

"You are a clumsy specimen, aren't you? Always stumbling over your own feet. At least this time you're dry." There was a peculiar merriment in his eyes as he bent over and scooped her up in his arms as if she were a rag doll.

"Put me down. I'm not a child." Her voice was on the edge of breaking, both from embarrassment and the closeness of his body.

"I'll put you down when I have you inside and can see how much damage you've done to your ankle this time."

Once inside, he placed her in the large chair next to the fireplace and removed her boot.

"Does that hurt?" he asked, gently moving her foot from side to side.

"No."

"Then I assume there are no broken bones. Wait here. I'll bring you a glass of port. It will help to steady you. Don't stand on your feet until that ankle has had a chance to rest a bit," he commanded.

While he was out of the room, Laura stood, testing the strength of her ankle. It felt perfectly all right to her. *I have to leave before he* returns, she thought as she quietly slipped her boot back on and made her way to the living room door.

"I see you're intent on sneaking off on me, Miss Bickford. Well, I won't detain you any longer."

As they faced each other, Laura noticed a look of abject defeat and uncertainty on Nat's face. It was a look she had never seen before in his eyes. His arrogance, his rudeness, his egotism—all that she could endure, but not this look of waning self-confidence. He was a man used to having his own way, always in total command of any situation. Now she was sapping the very essence from him and she hated herself for it. She lifted her warm amber eyes to meet his and held out her hand for the small glass of port, then went back to the comfortable chair.

Nat followed behind her, going to the fireplace. He rested his arms on the mantel and lowered his head to contemplate the flickering flames. She watched that familiar brooding expression steal across his face. She had seen it many times before at Evans Mansion.

She could see his shoulders tense as if a fiery struggle was raging deep within him. Time was suspended as the two people battled with their inner emotions in that quiet room. His shoulders heaved in resolution and she knew that what he was about to say required an enormous effort on his part. She wasn't sure she wanted to hear whatever he was about to say.

"Stay with me, Laura. I want you . . . I need you," he said softly, not turning to face her but steadily gazing into the fire.

Her heart leapt to hear his voice speak her given name with such tenderness and for the first time since they had met on the island. She realized it must have taken every bit of willpower he had to utter those words to her. He wasn't the kind of man who enjoyed pleading with a woman. Her few moments of elation were erased when the words themselves sank into her brain. Those words plunged her into an icy gloom, for they were Peter's words all over again, only said with a warmth and by a man she truly loved. But the sinking feeling increased as she knew she was the one being asked to make a commitment without receiving one in return.

She stared long and hard at those broad shoulders before leaving the chair and, with her heart screaming for her to stay regardless of the consequences, placed the half-finished glass of port on the table.

Nat spun on his heels at the imperceptible sound of the glass against the wooden table. She could see his endurance was at an end. He wanted an answer from her and he wanted an affirmative one. An incredible longing to yield to his tempting proposal coursed through her as his piercing blue eyes searched hers longingly for some sign of mutual need and consent. The need was there but not the will. She drew a strained breath, praying her voice wouldn't crack when she answered him.

"Mr. Harte, whatever else you may think of me, I never have, never will and never shall spend the night with any man who isn't my husband."

The blood throbbed against her temples as he closed the distance between them in two long strides.

"You fool!" he exclaimed, gripping her shoulders and pulling her to him lovingly.

His mouth came down on hers before she had a chance to speak. Spasmodic tremors danced up and down her spine and, in spite of her resolve, she found herself responding to his virile force. She had lost all will to resist him. Her eyes closed and her lips parted with eager acceptance of his tantalizing kiss. He crushed her closer and the hardened muscles of his legs pressing against hers sent her blood seething with raw desire throughout every atom of her being. Her senses screamed with a passion she never thought possible. She was diving headlong into a bottomless pit and she knew she had to stop it before it devoured her, leaving her completely helpless. She braced her hands on his chest and broke free of him.

"I'm not a toy for you to play with when the mood strikes you. I have feelings too and I'm not about to subject myself to your erratic whims. I'm sorry I ever came here and wish I had let Miss DeWitt bring the painting," she declared, her knees trembling. She was close to tears but refused to give him the satisfaction of seeing her reduced to a silly, whimpering schoolgirl. She swallowed hard then added, "And I'm not the fool you think I am."

"You are a little fool. A dear, sweet fool and I'm determined to have you and have you I shall." There was a taunting note in his voice and his blue eyes gleamed merrily as his arm shot out, his strong fingers curling gently around her wrist.

"Let go of me, you . . . you . . ." she stammered, her heart racing wildly, her nerve endings quivering.

"I don't think I will," he said mischievously, then added hoarsely, "Ever."

Laura stared at him quizzically. There was a softness in his eyes she couldn't fathom. Was she reading something into his words and countenance that really wasn't there? Was her imagination lending fact to her desires? Her stomach knotted as she furtively looked at him through lowered lashes. He cupped her chin and tilted her head back. She was transfixed as his fingers gently caressed her arched throat then trailed down to encircle her waist and draw her closer as his mouth mingled once again with hers in a sweet, deep joy. She quivered and a low, guttural moan of pleasure rumbled deep in her throat as his hands moved along her spine with delicate precision and exquisite insistence. Half mad with growing ecstasy, she offered no resistance but surrendered herself totally to the man who held and kissed her with such fevered passion. His lips left hers with a nibbling bite and a promise to return. He gazed long and hard into her pleading amber eyes.

"I have a sneaking suspicion you're not as immune to me as you pretend," he accused tenderly.

"Let me go," she implored, but there was a lack of conviction in her tone.

"Never."

"Mr. Harte . . ."

"Nathaniel," he corrected. "I don't think people would understand why you would call your husband Mister." A wide grin stole across his face as he watched her baffled reaction to his proposal. "Does the thought of being married to an arrogant rogue offend your sensibilities? You must admit I have at least one redeeming grace. I dance an excellent waltz."

The room was beginning to reel as Laura's mind and body went limp with shock. Her heart pounded relentlessly, draining her strength to speak as Nat took her head between his hands with loving tenderness and his eyes searched hers with an endearing longing.

"I can't fight it any longer, Laura. God help me but I love you. From the moment I saw you walk up the path to the mansion, I knew I would have a battle on my hands trying to keep from wanting you, loving you. All these months I've tried to stop, but it was impossible. I even went so far as to take out as many women as I could—anything to keep my mind off you, but it was all in vain. It only increased my desire and love for you." He drew a sharp breath. "Don't look at me like that, Laura. Tell me you'll marry me." His eyes narrowed perceptibly and his hands dropped to his sides when her silence continued. "Is it Courtney or your career you can't give up?"

"It's you I can't give up," she said at last, wildly flinging her arms around his neck. "Oh, Nathaniel, I love you so much. Not even in my wildest imaginings did I dare to hope you would love me too. You were always so aloof and indifferent."

"Automatic defense, my love. The thought of being in love with something other than art terrified me. I thought it would sap my artistic abilities, but loving you has augmented my creative powers to a pitch I've never known. Laura, I love you with a depth that makes my heart soar with creative powers I didn't know I possessed. I don't think I can make it without you now." He clung to her with fervent tenacity.

"I know this is all a dream and I'll wake up at any moment and find myself back in Brooklyn."

"I'll never let you go. But Courtney . . . what does he mean to you?"

"And Miss DeWitt? What does she mean to you?"

"There you go again," he laughed. "I'll break you of answering a question with a question if it takes me the rest of my life."

"I hope it does." She smiled up at him tenderly, love blatantly shining in her eyes.

He pulled her hard against him as his mouth caressed and nibbled at her softly parted lips. Laura tightened her arms around his neck and let loose with a passion she could no longer keep in check. It was a dangerous and devastating fervor that swept them along.

Reluctantly Nat held her from him and traced the back of his hand along the side of her cheek.

"You haven't answered my proposal of marriage yet."

"I would be proud and happy to become Mrs. Nathaniel Harte," stated Laura, love radiating from her every pore.

He gathered her up in his arms again and, as his lips teased along her slender neck, whispered in her ear, "I'm going to take you over to Mrs. Peale's for the night while I still have the willpower."

"I couldn't impose on Mrs. Peale like that. I hardly know the woman," she said, pulling away from him. "There must be a motel nearby."

"Mrs. Peale is a widow and would adore your company. Besides, if you were in a motel, I'd never leave it. No. Mrs. Peale's it is. In the morning we'll get the license, have the blood tests and do whatever needs to be done, then I'll drive you to the city and you can tell old Donaldson you're through."

"I can't do that!" she cried.

He stiffened. "You can't or you won't?"

"Both."

"I want you with me always . . . not cooped up in some museum."

Laura smiled and slipped her arms around his neck once again. "You know my work is important to me but it won't stand in the way of our happiness. Nathaniel, I'll ask Mr. Donaldson to give me some time off. It'll take a week at best to make the necessary arrangements. There are my parents and my friends to consider and I must call Hannah. I know she'll want to be here for the wedding," she said breathlessly.

His face softened as he hugged her to him. "I don't think I can wait a week."

"A week isn't a lifetime. We'll waltz through it."